REMEMBER ME

REMEMBER ME

BO HUSTON

Introduction by Dan Carmell

THE LIBRARY OF HOMOSEXUAL CONGRESS

NEW ORLEANS & NEW YORK

Published in the United States of America by The Library of Homosexual Congress
An imprint of Rebel Satori Press
www.rebelsatoripress.com

"ANYTHING GOES"
(Cole Porter)
copyright 1934 Warner Bros, Inc. (Renewed)
All Rights Reserved.
Used by permission.

Cover photo Bo Huston, by Robert Giard. Robert Giard Papers. Yale Collection of American Literature, Beinecke Rare Book and Manuscript Library. Copyright The Estate of Robert Giard; used by courtesy of Jonathan Silin.

ISBN: 978-1-60864-392-9

When near your death a friend
Asked you what he could do,
'Remember me," you said.
We will remember you.
    —Thom Gunn, *Memory Unsettled*

Introduction

by Dan Carmell

I have a strong memory of the first time I saw Bo, in late 1987. It was across a crowded, smoke-hazed room, the third-floor attic of a parsonage, in a room with currents and billows of cigarette smoke. That haze softened every outline and provided some further anonymity for whoever was talking. Bo was weaving toward the coffee pot, cigarette in hand. He was unshaved and looked very scruffy and I was immediately interested. I didn't know who he was, whether he was queer. I was very moody and distant that night, most nights then, and probably I ran off as everyone dispersed.

I heard about Bo first from friends, then I met him a few weeks later. We quickly started hanging out and I was just captivated by this savvy guy who had a New York City attitude and had gone to an elite college. I was 26—so was he. I was on the rebound from a relationship that never gelled and so was Bo. He'd been to San Francisco the previous winter, with a friend, a friend he was in love with, a friend who was unavailable sexually and emotionally. Now he was back to make a life here.

I've read scraps of Bo's journals from those early months and recently a close New York friend of Bo's shared a letter from Bo from just that period and it rang true to his journals—feeling lost, but feeling something different, something brighter in San Francisco, freedom from old haunts and habits. Bo was ready to start again.

Bo Huston was born Paul Richard Huston in Chagrin Falls, Ohio, June 10, 1959. He was born just a few weeks after me, smack in the safe nest of the middle class, sure that anything was possible, if pursued with some detachment. Bo's parents were both attorneys and fairly prominent in their community. Lu and Jim supplied their kids puzzles and challenges, took them on holidays abroad, and made for a house where books and music and conversation were encouraged. There's no question that the first sparks from Bo's mind were nurtured at home. But Bo's view of an eternally questionable, unsettled personal landscape also dates from his childhood. Bo was close to both his parents and I saw up-close how much they liked him, his dad especially. They supported Bo throughout his years with me, financially and emotionally. It was their assistance, along with SSI, that allowed Bo the time and freedom to write.

It was while Bo was in high school that he first had sex with men, older men that he sought out in parks, quick sexual things. It was when Bo was writing *The Dream Life* that he told me this and he was very clear in categorizing these experiences as positive. As we talked about young/old relationships, I learned again that Bo was more flexible than me, more willing to challenge certainties and allow for individual experience. Bo was a sensual person and he could give himself to up to ecstasy in a way I could not. Sex in Bo's novels is sometime awkward, never especially torn-jock strap sexy, but Bo's sensuality still informs those scenes, if in a slanting, sideways manner.

Bo's father told me how amused Bo was to go to the most expensive college in the country in 1977, Hampshire College in Massachusetts—an early indication of Bo's fascination with privileged people. The world opened up for Bo in college. That's when Paul became Bo, in his first or second year. A Hampshire friend told me it was a conscious, calculated effort to reimagine himself. Hampshire is where Bo met Tom Joplin, who taught film, and his partner Mark Massi. Imagine, 1978 or so, a gay man teaching film in the most subversive way he could—of course Bo was drawn to Tom. Tom brought Vito Russo to Hampshire to lecture. Those lecture notes, as I understand it, became *The Celluloid Closet*, which was something of a bible for Bo's understanding and approach to film, and ultimately, his writing.

After college, cocaine and then heroin took Bo into an increasingly bleak corner and made writing fragmentary or impossible. Bo got clean and quickly started writing again—I've found his film and play reviews in a New York City gay weekly, a free entertainment guide called *Michael's Thing*, circa 1986. They're cogent and smart. They show a bit of the wit and malice that seasons his fiction and later reviews in San Francisco's gay newspapers.

Bo had a great capacity for intimate relationships, was great fun in social settings in sly, rebellious ways, and people I barely knew adored him. In my mind's eye I see him with his cigarette, the TV possibly on mute, on the phone, occasionally rolling his eyes for my amusement, more often waving away the cigarette smoke and sipping tea. This was the Bo I adored quite completely. I was so content to be in his company, to be close to him at night. We'd be reading and I'd look up and he'd be looking at me from across the room, or I at him when he glanced up. We were both insecure, both afraid of love withdrawn or rejected. Bo's favorite memory of me, he said in his final weeks, was the night in 1988 when I threw down my gloves at the corner of Van Ness and Market, because Bo had danced with someone I had a jealous past with. Midnight in the rain—we were young!

Bo and I were together for almost six years. It was forever for him — someone told me afterwards. The last year of Bo's life, he got interested in Vedantic literature. Bo had met twice with the Swami who presides over that onion-domed Victorian on the way to the Golden Gate. I am not sure what he took from that, but when I hinted to Bo that if he could, I hoped he would wave at me from the great beyond. Bo looked me dead in the eye and said, "You too may have delusions." Bo was unwilling to hide behind illusions at the end.

I watched Bo reach out to publishers and editors. I watched him struggle with inattentive agents, all back in the age of typewriters and faxes. He wrote into the night and I woke to overflowing ash trays—but I did finally train Bo to fall asleep without the TV on.

Bo wrote four volumes of fiction over about five years. He had time to forge relationships with other writers and to support the OutWrite conferences and the Out/Look Quarterly that gave queer writers a new forum and increased visibility. Seeing his work in print wasn't just compensation for the time he didn't write, it was a promise kept.

Which brings us to this reissue of his first novel, *Remember Me*. Across Bo's college years and twenties, his closest bonds were with women and it appears that started at Hampshire College. Charlotte, or rather the woman who served as a model for Charlotte in the novel, was one of these college friends. Like Bo, Charlotte took part in the wide range of progressive instruction there; like Bo, Charlotte made what seemed like the natural move to New York City sometime in the early 1980s, and like Bo, Charlotte's focus shifted from words and art to drugs. About the time Bo entered rehab, Charlotte fled the city for her rural mountain home, after which they lost touch.

For me, *Remember Me* is very much about Bo's desire to capture the essence of his relationship with the real-life Charlotte, to understand what happened for her and why she retreated from life. Bo identified very deeply with Charlotte and all the characteristics he gave the novel's Charlotte. Bo chose to close the story without death or disaster, without resolution, but with a transcending experience. That speaks to Bo's experience and expectations for himself. Not closure, but completion.

Bo was largely well until early 1993. I recall seeing him in a band of sunlight in our Bernal Heights home that January, dancing a little jig in his happiness that *The Listener: A Novella and Four Stories*, was on the way to being published. Just five months later, wracked by pain and with a failing body, Bo chose when he would go. He said his goodbyes and made his final edits to a piece published posthumously, in Thomas Avena's *Life Sentences: Writers, Artists, and AIDS*. His ashes are scattered (quite illegally) at Land's End in San Francisco, where he loved to go for various types of inspiration.

It was on Castro Street Bo and I found the beads he is wearing in the photo on this cover. We were at that crazy intersection of Market and 17th. It was 1990 and there was no cure for AIDS, just AZT, which I had fought to make available. I had marched and protested and been arrested, for a drug that didn't do enough and had severe side effects but that's all we had. It was a sunny day and the community was defiantly alive. Bo and I were out and about -how blissful it felt to be with someone I adored and who loved me back.

There were street vendors working the sidewalks and we stopped to look at the bead work laid out by an older man, a gay hippy who was probably in his 60s, as I am now. He radiated something like a knowing serenity and Bo and I both felt something beneficent in his attention to us. We bought two similar strings of beads and put them on each other. They instantly symbolized something like wedding rings for us. That gay elder could feel it as well. From that point on, we wore them constantly.

When Bo was ill in his final months, he didn't wear his beads, but on the night of his death, I asked him to put them on and showed him the beads on my neck. I told Bo that after he was gone, I would switch the beads, so he would have mine and I his. I did that, and wore his for many years. Unstrung, I know just where they are and it's surely time I start wearing them again.

Original Dedication

– for Dan Carmell –

Summer

One

I know that death is merely a rumor. I pay it no mind. Disappearance is the real dilemma.

Passed that factory building again this morning on my walk. Women were lined up outside by the rusty gate—an uneven line, clusters of two and three. They wore heavy coats and gloves. A man was selling coffee and rolls. His cart squeaked a rhythm. The women were laughing—loud, mean laughter.

What was the name of that fussy old schoolteacher, whose face always got so red when she was mad? I must ask Charlotte.

This morning, the sun was layered with mist; the air was cool, damp. Next to a boarded up doorway, not far from where the women waited to be let in, I saw that pile of gloppy stuff again. It consists of twigs and paper, mud, ash, bits of glass and brick. I do not venture too close—I am afraid, I think, to know what it really is. The colors are brown, green, yellow, and it looks, from a distance, to be hard and caked with dirt. Every day on my walk I see this gloppy stuff, and its consistency and color change.

I stopped for a smoke, in front of the old Five-And-Dime. In the window was my reflection, fused with toy trucks, greeting cards, aluminum crutches and plastic flowers. I am a thin man, wearing one of those old-fashioned fedoras, brown and grey clothes, the expression on my unshaven face so somber and humorless. I look like someone children would run from. But, I am not somber and humorless, not at all!

So, as I continued my walk, I contemplated again my odd stubbornness about shaving. Most men shave every day, in the morning. My father always did. Even now, at thirty years old, I stall, avoid the soap and blades, and when two or three days have gone by I am amazed to see the bristle on my chin and cheeks. It is still a surprise to me, I guess, that I am grown up.

Mr Hornstein was just opening his store as I passed. I got Charlotte her "supplies," that is, the bandages and cream for her burns. And then, at the side of the store, I watched Hornstein's handsome son, David, unloading their old truck. David must know I moon over him as he heaves boxes and sweats and pushes that thick black hair away from his eyes. But, he pretends he does not see me. That's the game.

I took one of those wooden fruit crates; it will be perfect as a spice rack. Charlotte hates when I bring garbage home.

▼

Charlotte has been having terrible, feverish dreams lately, and calls out in her sleep. In my own room, I am awakened by a quick shout, and then can hear her as she turns on all the lights and makes her way through the halls and rooms of our house until she is exhausted. I hate to see her in this torturous battle between sleep and wakefulness, but there is nothing I can do for her.

I listen to her recount the dreams in the mornings, as we are eating crackers and drinking tea and smoking at our kitchen table.

"At first the whole thing is funny," she says. "We're on a boat, you and me and William Burroughs."

"William Burroughs is with us?"

"Right, and he's very quiet. He's sullen, he won't communicate."

"Yes, I see."

"And then I spy something floating past our boat...something white...paper, or cloth...and I reach for it, and when my fingers touch the surface of the water, I am burned, very badly burned, all brown and wrinkled up."

"Yes, I see."

Her dream had her suddenly inside a dark green and misty jungle. She said could not see the sky. She said she felt at peace. And then a sly monkey stole her cigarettes.

▼

We were born in the shadows of all the wars. Raised with doubt, flattered and galled her whole life, Charlotte retreated finally into imperviousness and her moods. Her words and tone are never bitter, though. Perhaps she is happy.

She will say: "Go on, oh, go for your walk. I know you love your walks. Don't worry at all about me." She sees that I am restless as my nervous hands turn over a matchbook. Sometimes Charlotte possesses a magnificent generosity and sincerity, something distinctly feminine and confident.

And so encouraging: "I thought your little story was just absolutely brilliant. A *brilliant* thing."

"Oh, thank you Charlotte. I liked it. They changed the middle, though."

"Stupid magazine editors. How dare they?"

Charlotte used to get out once a week to see Dr Klein, and she would tell me everything that happened: her journeys through the town to and from his office and all that was said in the sessions.

"I think Frank is very lonely," Charlotte told me. She called her therapist Frank. "Of course, you can't know for sure...he's very discreet, not at all forthcoming about his own life. I guess they're not supposed to be. But, I do have this impression...you know, I'll be talking about things, about my mother or whatever, about my scars, and Frank's eyes just get this kind of glaze over them, so distant. I'm sensitive to these things. And I keep talking so as not to embarrass him. He's lonely, I know. I can see it."

She began these sessions last year and quit them after a few months. Her specific problem was that she could not or would not leave home; she had no motivation or desire to interact in any way at all with the world outside our rooms on Station Road.

We live in an unkempt one-storey house, barely more than a railroad flat. There is a fireplace with green and white tiles and a stained mahogany mantle. The furniture comes mostly from Charlotte's family and it is weathered, but some of the pieces have charm. Our silver and china belonged originally to Charlotte's mother, as well.

The rooms are cluttered with stacks and shelves of favorite books with raggedy covers, musty blankets draped over chairs, shaded lamps. We have several cheap china figurines, bought in junk shops or yard sales;

one is a boy with a drum and a chipped, fading pink smile. I do not like this boy, but he has sat on our window sill so long now that I am used to him. I would miss him if he broke.

There are many framed pictures on the walls; none is of family, none has anything to do with Charlotte or me—they are clippings from newspapers or photographs hastily ripped from magazines and books, images of murderers (Charlotte's passion) and movie stars (mine). Years ago, I did come across a photo I couldn't resist: black and white of someone named Tad, a naked boy with a huge, dangling dick, long hair and glassy, stoned eyes. This picture hangs above the bathroom sink.

The radiators clank and hiss, the linoleum in the kitchen has begun to curl, plaster is cracking at the corners of the ceiling. I used to gaze about the house—especially in the morning when the sun was bright across the dull wood floor—a little wistfully, guilty, nervous, as though the place seemed to represent nothing but a sour job to be done. Now, it is hardly even noticeable to me that every window sill is coated with a layer of grey dust, that the stuffing rolls out of the corners of our chairs, that surfaces and corners and cracks are covered with lost scents, past breezes and chills and moisture—air and time. A tarnished, loose doorknob serves as an ominous reminder that our sturdy, winning little house is simply beyond repair. It will never be clean.

Charlotte sits within it, or amidst it all, without a blink or a shrug, unattached to any idea of how the place should be kept. It seems to me, when I think about it, that we've descended rather sadly from our upbringing. We were not raised to allow newspapers to pile in the corner or let a hinge on a cupboard go unmended. Our orderly families cared something about flowers arranged in vases and windows without streaks, counters free of dust, rugs shaken, and bowls with fruit placed exactly in the center of the table. Now, the hall light bulb has been burned out for weeks. I do not change it, though it irritates me every night, and Charlotte seems not to notice. Charlotte says—and this is so like her—that by firelight, our house has no shortcomings at all.

At first she bullied herself into walking to her appointment with Dr Klein. When that became too unpleasant—she claimed she could not catch her breath—she would call for a taxi. Finally, one day, the blue and white cab pulled in front of our house and Charlotte simply lowered the

4

shades.

"I hope you won't be mad with me," she said that night. "I do know things are wrong with me, really, I understand all that. I just can't...I just can't. Will you forgive me?"

I do not think her seclusion is really caused by a fear of people so much. I believe that Charlotte shies away from decisions of any kind, that for Charlotte there is some mysterious pain in all considerations: whether to turn right or left, whether to buy a blue or yellow hat, whether to post her letters first or stop at the bank or have her lunch. Those common actions which measure people's days confound and repel her. What is so extraordinary and sad about Charlotte, and yet so dear, is that she has arranged her life as to have no choices.

▼

Horrible walk today.

Pages from someone's notebook were strewn across the street and sidewalk, blown by a soft breeze, fluttering, alighting crazily against a car, a mailbox, a lamppost. Anonymous sad or angry reflections about love are out there now, the daily news of someone's life, the private prayers.

Three schoolgirls in crisp new dresses marched like soldiers, arm in arm, chanting, and kicked those pages with their new shoes. How cruel.

As I followed the curve in the road, I saw that snooty Mrs Coffee was in her usual dilemma: she insists on driving her enormous shiny black Cadillac around town, even to the post office or the butcher; but the roads here are narrow and uneven, and she is hard-put then to turn the thing around towards home. Other cars are forced to wait, pedestrians are pushed into doorways, as she, wearing dark glasses, waving her cigarette, swears and fumes in her struggle. Once, she knocked over a stop sign. Mrs Coffee has been divorced three or four times and is very well off. She wears a huge blonde wig. When we were teenagers, Charlotte and I titillated ourselves with the notion that Mrs Coffee was a transsexual.

That pile of muck has grown: cigarette butts and a bent beer can have been added. A tiny brown sparrow danced on it and then flew off. I pass this pile daily now, curious. When will someone clear this garbage? Why is it so passively accepted? And I am attracted to its progress: how enormous, how revolting, how powerful can this mess become?

On my morning walks, I take giant steps. To independence, perhaps; to a secure and serene sense of myself... away from the indecision and gloom, the terminality which characterizes poor Charlotte. A slow mid-morning walk, whatever the weather, is my preparation for the day when one of us, Charlotte or I, dies and the other is left alone.

▼

Charlotte and I have always been together. My family's house was two doors down from hers. Our mothers drank coffee at each other's kitchen tables, and our fathers stood in each other's yards, discussing things. She had an older sister, Annie. We both adored Annie, and sought her attention. My memory-picture of Annie has her sitting on the steps of the school gossiping with two or three girlfriends, all wearing plaid skirts.

Charlotte and I kissed one grey, smoky summer day on her back steps. When we were ten, we had a crushing fight on our way home from school and would not speak to each other and were miserable and stubborn. I was the most stubborn, I suppose, for it was Charlotte who ended the feud one week later. She called to me as I walked alone. I stopped, she ran up and stood facing me. "Oh, I'm sorry. I am really sorry. Let's not fight. Let's always be friends." I gave a short nod and we walked the rest of the way home together. I kept my head lowered, embarrassed at the scene and the weeklong silence. I remember that Charlotte just hummed, skipped a little; for her, all was repaired and healed, back as it should be.

When we were twelve, Charlotte's mother got sick, and through the green, wet summer the grownups stepped cautiously, spoke in low tones, wore worried looks. The night her mother died, a penny hit my window, then another. I looked out into the misty dark, and there was Charlotte, her dead mother's old fur coat over her nightgown, standing on our porch beneath the yellow light. "Let me up?" she called.

I burned Charlotte when we were teenagers. Her legs have scars and she says they still sting. We had driven my father's car to the park for a cookout. We brought charcoal and a grill to make steaks. We were laughing and singing songs from Broadway shows, forgetting the words and making up our own. Somehow, I got kerosene on Charlotte's skirt—a cotton skirt with green and blue squares which I never will forget—and she was too close to the fire. She twirled and jumped frantically, ran in circles; and rather than shrieking, she emitted a soft, high sound, like the crazy final note of a song. I chased her, crying for her to stop so I could put out the flames. As we raced to the hospital in the giant blue car, tears streamed steadily down my face, and I whispered a husky incantation: I'm sorry, I'm sorry, I'm sorry.

Charlotte's breathing was heavy, rapid, and she pressed a blanket against her lap. "*That,*" she said, "was incredible. The most exhilarating few moments I will ever have."

Then, I attributed Charlotte's shocking remark to some sort of melodramatic delirium; today, I believe it was just the truth. She smooths cream over those ancient scars, dresses them with bandages sometimes. It is a queer ritual that I do not understand. When she touches her legs, it is as if she is handling something fragile and rare, but ugly, something she does not really love. Charlotte will not believe that her burns have healed.

Charlotte gets thinner each week. She doesn't eat properly, and I am not the sort of person to pester her. When I go on my walks, she watches the soap operas on our old portable black-and-white television, delighted with the squalid details of sexual abuse, multiple personalities, divorce and drinking and disease. Charlotte has always been a collector of gruesome, tragic stories. She seems genuinely moved by these dramas, though. "Poor woman," Charlotte says about one of her afternoon characters. "It's amazing she can still be a nurse and raise her twins, after all she's been through! Her husband was a surgeon, but then he became an awful alcoholic and now his hands shake."

▼

Last night I lay on the sofa, covered by two blankets. The kitchen light remained on, casting an amber cone, and Charlotte's radio played softly from her room: sweet flutes and a man singing in German. The battered, yellowing window shade blew and tapped the sill. The door shifted in its frame with a creak. It's as though, each night, our old house draws back, sighs, settles itself.

7

To be sure, Charlotte stays awake long after the house and I are still. She writes a letter, or reads through those books piled on her bed, or sorts through her photographs and clippings.

I felt absolute comfort last night, with those sounds, in these rooms, a feeling of being safe at home. Charlotte is my family.

She slipped into the front room. Believing I was asleep, she quietly moved to the bookcase and opened its glass doors, strained in the dimness searching for a particular book, pulled out several and stole them to her enormous bed, which is, I suppose, where Charlotte feels safe at home.

▼

This morning, I was reading the *Dear Margie* advice column of the paper aloud, and Charlotte and I were laughing. "Confidential to Superior: A girl eventually loses her looks, you know..." Charlotte was sitting on top of her photo album, to make the glue stick. And that song which seems to me so pathetic and untrue—*You Always Hurt The One You Love*—was playing on the radio. The door buzzer sounded. Charlotte and I looked at each other, timid, almost guilty, exactly as we looked when that fussy teacher caught us smoking as children.

We turned the radio down and I let in our visitor. Charlotte's Aunt Kaye is a tall, emaciated, stooped woman in her forties, very curt, dressed always in a dark print dress and a hat, with an oversized pocketbook hanging from her elbow. Her face is sharp and white, and she does her thin lips with a pale pink.

"Morning, morning," she said. Charlotte said: "Morning, Aunt Kaye," and rose to get some tea. With Charlotte in the kitchen, Aunt Kaye looked at me, brow arched, and mouthed silently the question: How is she? I squinted, as though I could not make out her words—I do not like to play conspirators with Aunt Kaye—and then Charlotte returned with a tea tray.

"Oh, goodness," Aunt Kaye said, cheerful once again and too loud. "I don't have much time, Charlotte, dear. Just here to have you sign a few things." Aunt Kaye is in charge of the financial accounts. She pulled a set of onion-skin papers from her pocketbook and unclipped them. Charlotte sat beside her on the sofa. Aunt Kaye began explaining various paragraphs—here was an addition, this means that—and telling Charlotte not to worry over these little things, which Charlotte certainly did not. She signed each page without the slightest interest and smiled at her aunt as she handed back the pen.

"Well, that's settled, then. Fine, dear." Aunt Kaye sipped her tea and glanced about the room, wide-eyed, as though alarmed by our home. Her high-pitched voice startled us then: "Don't you ever like to get out, Charlotte?"

Charlotte smiled, patient and amused. "No, I'm not much for that."

"Well, that's too bad, then," said Aunt Kaye, wistfully, looking at a corner of the ceiling. "Pretty girl like you could be out *doing* things, *going* places...."

▼

We ate early tonight and were smoking and having coffee at the table before clearing away.

Charlotte said: "I remember walking down our street with my sister when I was a little girl. Supper time. Evening, like this. The evening world, I think, is so much nicer than the world of day or night. The sun just setting. A chilly mist. Love does not seem so remote or sad.... So, Annie and I walked down our street, that winding street, past your house and the trees we used for tag, and the back of the school. The houses got a little bigger, you recall, where the people had more money. They were set back from the walk behind gates and shrubs. Do you remember the name of that big dog we were so afraid of? But, we teased it, we provoked it!

"Annie was just so lovely and calm. Nothing bothered Annie, she always was pleasant, always smiling.

"To the end of the street, to the rich people's houses, and then we turned and started back. And Annie said: 'Just think, Charlotte, that behind all of these lighted windows are people, families like ours. Boys and girls and grownups. And they all have different thoughts and feelings, as we do, and things they like or don't like.' The church in town chimed its bells, then. Annie said: 'Think of all the lighted windows in all the houses on all the streets...the towns, and the apartment buildings in the big cities, and farms...and different countries around the world. All these

9

people sit down to their suppers every night. So many people, living their lives!' she said.

"And I did not say anything to Annie. I was only a little girl, and I was amazed. Annie said: 'The world is very big, Charlotte. And it has been going on a long time.' Then, I was frightened. And I felt ashamed, too, but could not have said why."

Tears stood still in Charlotte's eyes. Her face was red, but she was smiling. I sipped some coffee and Charlotte walked around the room, then came behind me and put her hands on my shoulders. "I *am* sorry," she whispered. I said nothing. "You remember our street, don't you? And my beautiful sister?" I touched her fingers gently.

Two

This town is nestled between two small hills along the river. Patches of green and brown are threaded by the railroad tracks. The tiny houses, a steeple, a train station, a whitewashed flagpole in its center make it seem like a toy town that one need not take too seriously.

There is a row of grim storefronts on Center Street—a hardware, a grocery, a butcher. A grey stone church, the firehouse and a post office stand cracked and tilting like gravestones; and they are proud structures, signals to this precinct of many terrible and astonishing years. Above the roofs, plumes of clouds make shapes for the children to trace: mean faces and angel's wings. It is an inscrutable town.

Charlotte and I live on the outskirts. We are just up the hill from the train station, close to the river, in sight of the factory where many of the town people work. Peerless Manufacturing Company, it is called. When I was small I asked my father what peerless meant, and was told "superior." Consequently, I carried a mental picture of the factory owner, named Peerless: elderly, rather sweet, but untouchable and remote and lonely. Lionel Barrymore Peerless, standing behind the enormous leaded windows, his pipe sending those bursts of sooty clouds directly through the smokestack.

The Turners moved into the drab green house at the end of Station Road a few years ago. From the wicker chair where I sit on our back porch I can see into their yard, overgrown with brownish weeds. The leaves of past autumns are pushed against the rusted fence. The youngest of the Turner children is a girl, not over five years old, and she suffers from a bone disease: she is fragile, undersize, and must wear a cap in the sun. The little girl chases awkwardly after her brothers and sisters, but cannot keep up with their games. When she stumbles and falls onto the moist grass, her mother hurries from the house, scolding the other children, who stare solemnly at their sister. The little sick girl only blinks,

11

too confused to cry.

Mrs Turner's life certainly seems a hard one. That apron she wears all day and into the evening has a faded yellow flower print. Her husband travels. When he arrives home, once or twice a month, she will step out onto the porch and watch him walk up the road from the station. She smiles, but there is nothing in that smile or the tense lift of her shoulders that shows true relief or any pleasure. Mr Turner's hat will be pushed back on his head, his tie and collar loosened; they exchange a kiss.

All of those Turner children are soon gathered round the father, pulling at his trousers and coat, laughing. He is all exhaustion, she is struggling patience. Mr Turner will bring a special gift from his pocket for the sick girl, something small, a toy animal or a picture book, and hand it to her, kiss her cheek.

In the evenings, their downstairs windows blink silver and blue fight from the television—I imagine Mr Turner dozes off to it. I can see Mrs Turner finishing up her work in the kitchen. From the children's room on the second floor come thuds, playful shrieks, doors closing and laughter.

I feel so keenly the weariness of Mr and Mrs Turner, and pity their misfortune which is frighteningly ordinary; it is not made of catastrophe and trauma, but of dull days, tedious jobs to be done, children to look after; both have pains in their joints which will only get worse.

Sometimes I try to tell Charlotte about the Turners, but she does not like to hear about them. "Families are spooky," she says. Just five years after her mother died, Charlotte's father killed himself. He put a shotgun to his temple. It was the summer before our last year of high school. We were walking home from the movie in town—it was Hitchcock's *The Birds*. I loved it. Charlotte despised it: the premise was preposterous, the scenery all looked fake, and she could not possibly take seriously any actress called 'Tippi'; and so we were arguing as we turned onto our street, passed the empty, blond-brick school building and its playground, and as we approached our houses, Charlotte abruptly stopped walking. I was a few steps ahead of her, with my mouth open, dumb, staring, and felt a tightness in my chest as though my lungs were too full. A police car was parked in the drive of Charlotte's house, an ambulance was on the front lawn, crooked, it looked like it might tip over. The red lights of these vehicles were spinning flashes, but there was no sound, there was a dead stillness. We walked forward, very slowly, noiselessly.

Two ambulance men brought Charlotte's father through the front door and rushed him into the back of their car, sped away—and still it all seemed done in silence, in an odd deference to a dead man's lunacy, as when a drunk at a party throws a tantrum and no one knows what to say, no one will even breathe.

Aunt Kaye was there that day, and afterwards came to manage things and take care of Charlotte. Annie was by then established in the city, working for a magazine and engaged to Dr Rosenberg; but she returned home. It seems now like another life, a dream life. Charlotte took to wearing a dirty red knit beret and talked tirelessly about sex as though she really knew. Even then she had that giant, howling laugh.

Our adolescence was made of drama, isolation and waiting—to get out, to grow up. Tragedy was possible, but disappointment was inconceivable. Nothing but grand gifts awaited us because, as Charlotte insisted, we were gifted.

I would be a writer, of course, and would probably teach at Harvard or Oxford and would fall in love with one of my students and travel the world. Charlotte did not have such concrete goals for herself. She lived in moody dreams of sensations she needed to have, or to avoid. She knew she'd live at the ocean when she was an old lady. She also knew she would never get pregnant and if she did she'd have an abortion without a second thought or a wasted moment. She was attracted, at different times, to journalism and prostitution, to law school (but she would not want to practice) and photography. A favorite idea was that she would move to New Orleans, change her name and open a restaurant or a laundry. And never be heard from again.

Emotions were charged and brittle between Charlotte and her sister at home. Annie had become chic, slender—everything about her signaled competence and resentment. Charlotte, though, was churlish, tall and handsome, and her black eyes showed her just itching for recklessness. Also, it turned out that Charlotte's share of her father's considerable estate was very much larger than Annie's, I suppose because Charlotte was a child, and Annie was already out of college, about to be married.

They argued constantly, and when they were silent, misunderstanding and distrust settled between them, taut, impenetrable. Charlotte stopped going to school. We would walk there together in the mornings, but by lunch Charlotte was gone, had disappeared, leaving an empty desk in each of her classes. "I can't remember one thing I've learned in all these years of school so far," she told me. "No math or spelling or anything else. It's a waste." She spent the afternoons walking around our town, to the river, to the woods.

"You were absent again today," Annie declared.

"I wasn't absent. I was present."

"Are you saying you were in school today?"

"Well, maybe I wasn't in school, but I wasn't absent. I was somewhere else and if I was somewhere else then I was present."

"Well, you weren't where you were *supposed* to be," Annie said bitterly, holding her breath, and then muttered: "Petulant little bitch."

One evening, just before supper, I stood at Charlotte's kitchen door. Annie was on the phone, frowning and fiercely smoking a cigarette. I kept quiet, my hands clasped behind me, intimidated into politeness, as I always was. Annie noticed me. "Charlotte's not here," she practically barked. "And I don't know where she is." She turned her head and said into the phone: "It's nobody, just that friend of Charlotte's."

I walked through the still neighborhood, and found Charlotte leaning against the mailbox at the end of our street. We were silent for a few moments, and then Charlotte said: "I'm not looking forward to summer at all. I don't even want to be here for summer. I'm bored of this town, sick to death of it. I should go be a prostitute in Europe." We shared a cigarette, walked through the school yard, then back home. Deep down, I must have thought it was I Charlotte was despising. She brought me inside—we walked past Annie and the sisters said nothing, did not look at each other—and up to her room.

"Okay," said Charlotte. "Do you want to see what I've been doing lately?" Her grin was wicked, a confrontation.

At the bottom of Charlotte's untidy closet was a bag, which she emptied onto her bed. Paperback books, tubes of lipstick, pens, packets offlower seeds and lavender soap and a ball of yarn, greeting cards, magazines. I looked at these curious treasures and Charlotte was looking at me.

"I stole these," she said.

"All of this stuff, Charlotte?"

"Yes, all of it. I went into the Five-and-Dime one day last week. And I saw—what was it?—oh, this paperweight." She held up a brass ship. "So, just on an impulse, without thinking about it at all, I just stuck this ship in my coat pocket. And then I walked through the aisles, being very casual. And I smiled at that bald guy who works the cash register. He said, 'Why aren't you in school today Charlotte?' and I told him my class went on a field trip and I couldn't go. He said, 'Why couldn't you go with your class?' I told him because my father had just died so recently, I was needed at home. And he got very red and embarrassed. I said goodbye to him and walked out of the store, and then faster down the street, and then ran home. What a feeling it was. I imagined being caught, someone grabbing my arm and pulling me away and the police being called, Annie just completely outraged and Aunt Kaye hurt and tragic about it all."

I was appalled and impressed by this recklessness. "But, you didn't get caught?" I whispered.

"No! That's what's so amazing. So, I keep going back, every day, even a couple times a day, and pick up some little thing, chat with that bald guy, and walk out. It's like I've discovered a special hidden talent. The trick is to behave as though you're entitled to something. And if you're entitled to something, you just take it, no fuss, no worry. It's yours. And I know I'll *never* get caught."

This logic troubled me. Ever reasonable and cautious, I shook my head: "You might, Charlotte. You might go along, stealing things, and everything's fine, and then one day you'll get caught. You won't be expecting it...."

She turned from me, opened her window so she could light a cigarette and wave the smoke into the cool night air. "Don't be so serious," she ordered. I felt very childish then, sitting on the bed that was almost like my own bed, a place I'd shared with her on summer nights, slept and sweated in ever since I could remember; now it was covered with spoils of a different, distant Charlotte. I was afraid for her, seeing this chaotic course of lying and stealing.

So, it was then I first felt a difference between us, a separation which hit me as such a cruel blow; the tender, dear side of Charlotte was edged with an audacity I could not comprehend. I was afraid and delighted.

15

And where did her sense of entitlement originate? How did she ever develop that shrug as a way to confront sorrow?

Some years later, when my mother was killed in a plane crash, I realised that funerals were a great part of our journey together. At these events, I am terrified and anxious. Charlotte has a standard uniform for such occasions: her dark blue suit with a white blouse, her mother's exquisite string of pearls. During the service, she will look off at the tops of the trees, at the grass blowing along the hillside, away, not at the minister or the gravestone or the coffin or me. She is so lovely, so distant, like a girl in a corner of a ballroom.

Is death, then, the source of Charlotte's blessed and infuriating pathos?

Charlotte said to me once: "It is a heartbreaking and strange thing to be an orphan." But, I have seldom heard her say much about her parents. Sometimes I think I recollect them more vividly than she does. She cherishes the photographs, has pasted and arranged and examined them regularly for years now. She refers to her mother as "a bit of a beatnik" (which is not at all true). Her father she remembers as decent and kind, if rather weak.

But Charlotte sees varied, broad meaning in the orphan state. "It's like having a tragic flaw. It's like a baby born without an arm or a leg or something. Or a cat who's had its claws removed. It never can understand life as it was meant to. Something is always missing. Always incomplete. It has to compensate, because it is without the essential resources, what it needs to survive."

▼

There was nothing in the mail for me today. I have been expecting a letter from XXX Press, Inc. regarding my book. The post-mistress, Peg Pelliteer, sits behind a wire screen. She is unfriendly; she will begrudgingly push aside the detective or tabloid magazine she reads with pathetic voraciousness to deal with her patrons, and her blue-shadowed eyes blink a challenge. Her face recalls a cartoon horse from my childhood. When she hands over the mail addressed to me or Charlotte, and there is nothing from XXX Press, Inc., her lips are set tight, and I begin to imagine she feels deeply satisfied at my disappointment. When I get home, Charlotte watches my expression. I try to appear casual and unconcerned. What a silly game.

The train ride into the city takes only thirty minutes or so. We follow along the river, winding, curving, and then, always so suddenly, the city appears ahead: its tall buildings look like sticks with holes and tiny flags perched on top, bands of highway connect its ends, an icy blue of glass and steel. The city people's cigarette smoke and rotten attitudes form a pancake cloud above it all and, as it has since I was a little boy, it looks and smells like freedom to me.

I arrived ten minutes late for my clinic appointment. I sat off by myself, reading. The place is painted a weak mustard color and lined with folding chairs. Outdated magazines with their covers curled are tossed onto little end tables. I gave my name to the nurse, Steve. He is always so friendly, and I berate myself for not liking him; I can barely manage a lame smile. A tiny woman wearing rollers in her hair was in the waiting area trying to keep track of four toddlers; she could not stop one of them from bawling, and I tried not to show my irritation. My doctor is not much older than I, though his hair is thinning. He has a wonderful, white smile and an appealing, long face. He looks exceptionally clean and healthy. He strikes me as unusually passive for a professional man. Dr Fred Decker. I have been seeing this man twice a month for almost a year, now, and still do not address him by his first name.

"So, what's been going on?" he asked me—his usual beginning.

"Oh, I've been fairly well, Dr Decker. I've been fine."

As he looked over the lab reports on my blood and his notes from our last appointment he asked particulars: "Sleeping?"

"Yes."

"Any shortness of breath, trouble walking up hills?"

"No. A little. Not really."

"How about eating?"

"Not much appetite, I'm really not eating much." I make this statement each time I see Dr Decker, and he always raises an eyebrow; he really is a very attractive man. "I forget to eat, sometimes, and sometimes I just can't think what I want."

"You should force yourself to eat." He glanced over the record of my weight. "You are losing a few pounds every month, and that's not good at all."

Another routine interaction between Dr Decker and myself is my questions about new treatments I've heard of. This morning I had written a note to myself on the back of an envelope, to be sure to inquire about a combination of Chinese herbs which I had read could bolster the immune system, as well as a medication that is being tested in Denmark. Dr Decker nodded his head; full tests have not been made on either of these substances. He smiled, he shrugged just slightly. Dr Decker is fairly conservative, I think, and unexcitable. He hears of new drugs every day. Perhaps he has seen people try so many things and become discouraged, and seen hope just splintered by proud promises and quick death. What an extraordinary time this is—I think of those men with the long mustaches who traveled the countryside a hundred years ago selling patent medicines, snake oil, remedies for every ailment. The funny thing is that I never do press Dr Decker much. He is patient with me, I am patient with him. He knows more than I, presumably, but cannot possibly have the investment I do in my staying alive. I look in his intelligent, handsome eyes, I wonder about him. When he closes my file, does he think I will die someday soon?

Today, there was no need for me to take off my clothes, and for that I was grateful. I just hate to take off my clothes. "And how is the writing going?" Dr Decker wondered vaguely, as I was preparing to leave.

"I...yes...the book is finished."

"That's wonderful, really wonderful. It's a novel?"

"Yes."

He had pushed open the examining room door and was motioning to the nurse for the next file when he said: "See you next month," and smiled.

I am always stricken by the impulse, just before we leave, to say, "But, wait. Tell me. Am I going to survive?" I would not ask such a question, not risk that bewildering, charming shrug of his shoulders. I just struggled with my jacket and gloves and the big bag I am always carrying around, tried to scoot out quickly to allow for his next patient. Sometimes I feel I'm in his way.

▼

Charlotte has been in her cranky mood all day. When I left the house this morning to catch the train, she was rifling through boxes of crinkled papers and bent file folders, searching for something, and when Charlotte is searching for something, her single-mindedness, her intensity of purpose make her demanding and inconsiderate.

I returned this afternoon to find newspaper clippings arranged over nearly the whole floor of the front room, and Charlotte squatting in the center, smoking a cigarette, frowning. "There are so many bugs in the kitchen cabinet," she snapped at me, without even looking up. "That's true," I muttered, and stepped out onto the back porch. The sun was high, but layered with silver, wet mist. I took three deep breaths. That is my method for coping, my remedy for Charlotte's unpleasant moods which, after all, do not ever last too long.

For several weeks I have been getting headaches in the evenings, but I have not told Dr Decker. There is much I keep from him, and I don't know why. A queer, unsightly, very painful infection began on my foot a few weeks ago. And I have been nauseous lately. But I do not tell the doctor of these things.

I have never been a very responsible person. My father used to call me lazy, and Mother would say: "He isn't lazy, just preoccupied." But, I know I am not the best person for the job of taking care of myself. I swallow the medication sporadically, when I remember to. Sometimes I forget to go for my blood tests. I have missed doctor appointments. It would be tragic if I actually died because I was too lazy to fill a prescription, too meek to tell my doctor about a symptom.

Sitting in this shabby wicker chair on the back porch, the sun sets to a mild, comforting breeze. Charlotte is curled on the sofa inside, under an afghan her mother made. In an hour or so, we will debate about supper.

There is a cafe a few blocks from my clinic in the city. I went there today for coffee and sat alone at one of the outdoor tables.

Two young men were near me, drinking juice and eating pastries. Both had short blond hair and wore blue jeans and jackets, and both had sunglasses perched on their heads. One pulled out a notebook and opened it and was showing some papers to the other. They laughed about something, and they had broad grins showing white teeth. As they rose to leave the place, I focused on their identical perfect figures: round, tough butts and thick legs, strong shoulders and chests and necks, alluring mounds at the crotch, and such handsome faces. They strode down the street together. When they were out of my view, I was left with a clear and bitter sense of being inadequate and unhealthy. Or just apart.

Charlotte's response to her small experience in the world outside our house was to feel its desperation and cruelty, and then to deliberately retreat.

I believe longing is my demon, and it separates me so from Charlotte. She is not wishing to be healthy, to live elsewhere, for love or to make any kind of mark in the world. Charlotte's only wish has been to stay home, and it is granted, every day. She never longs to be someone else.

Three

Charlotte had spent a few months on her own, living in the city. She hated it, it confused and changed her. "People were always bumping into me, and I was afraid I'd get knocked down." But, of course, there was more to it than that.

We were sitting on her bed one night, both suffering from the merciless summer flu that was going around. Charlotte had balls of tissue on her lap. "It was too loud, too smoky, too fast," she said of the city. But I know there was more to it than that. Dr Klein had judged this period of her life to be the root of her predicament, the key to her condition. To Charlotte it's a sad, terrible dream, it's deep in the past.

There was a storm; the windows shook, which Charlotte loved. She had stuck candles in soda bottles round her room, and in their long, gold light, I watched her as she told me her story.

It was more than ten years ago, we were both eighteen. One of Charlotte's poems had been printed in a magazine. I was away at school, but I wrote to offer encouragement. Charlotte had lived in the same little room at her father's house all her life. She was very much excited by a long poem she was writing, and believed that in order to continue her work, she needed to move to the city.

There she shared a tiny and drafty two-room apartment with a girl named Lucy Williams on the third floor of a brownstone in one of those charming, crooked streets lined with trees roped to poles. There was a row of mailboxes in the black and white tiled vestibule, and the sight of her own name, above Apt. 3B, was exciting but terrifying too.

The roommate, Lucy, had ambitions to be a singer. She spent the days sleeping, the evenings dressing and making up and covering her wrists and neck with costume jewelry. Lucy stayed out at night, willingly swallowed up by cruel, loud laughter, bright yellow taxicabs, cigarette smoke, greedy men. Lucy would stumble up the stairs every morning, struggle with the key in the latch as though it were an unfamiliar door, waking Charlotte. She'd kick off her highheeled shoes, step out of some splendid dress, and report to Charlotte what had happened to her the previous night. Lucy Williams's chief area of expertise was men, and she tried to teach Charlotte: "If you just leave them alone, they'll say and do what you want them to."

It was during this cohabitation with Lucy Williams, Charlotte says, that she came to understand how much she did not like other females. Their hips were too wide; their bodies were like pin-cushions; and Charlotte could never take them seriously. She decided never to be jealous of a woman.

"I'm singing in a lounge bar this weekend," Lucy told Charlotte. "I'm so thrilled. Come hear me. Please come to hear me sing. And I'm changing my name. To Gale."

Charlotte could not get into the habit of using the name Gale; she continued to call her roommate Lucy, and Lucy would pretend she hadn't heard.

Charlotte's sister Annie and her Aunt Kaye had imposed a condition on her living in the city, that she learn some sort of trade. So, three days a week she went to a secretarial school to study shorthand and typing. One humid, miserable morning Charlotte pushed among the sour-faced strangers boarding the crosstown bus. She did not get a seat, of course, and had come to expect this hardship of standing against people, her shoulders hunched, the muscles in her arm burning from holding the strap. Seated in front of her was a pleasant-looking older woman wearing a blue suit and white gloves and with an elegant, meticulously styled puff of white hair. Seated on this woman's lap was a girl. In telling this story, Charlotte refers to her as The Toothpick Girl. The girl's age was not discernible, but she was no longer a child. Her elbows jutted out like marbles, her wrists were no bigger than two of Charlotte's fingers. Her head was average size, but perched on a brittle, narrow neck, like a puppet's head, too heavy. Her face was pale and gaunt, the eyes enormous. The Toothpick Girl had full, long blonde hair. Her mood seemed relaxed. She and the older woman companion chatted in low, calm tones.

Charlotte stared at the woman and The Toothpick Girl, feeling at once repelled and drawn, fascinated by more than the mysterious weak body or an unnamed disease. It was the simple relationship, one sitting on the other's lap, that kept Charlotte's attention riveted to the couple before her. What people will endure, Charlotte was thinking.

The Toothpick Girl noticed Charlotte staring. She leaned her puppet head against her woman friend's soft hair and whispered. The woman friend glanced tersely at Charlotte. "Well," said The Toothpick Girl, "I guess by now I'm used to being stared at."

Charlotte spent evenings in her back room, which was the plainer and smaller of the two. She'd sit on the edge of the narrow bed, the typewriter before her on a wooden stool. Her room faced an alley, and below her was a window, always dark, and above, another one, with a bottle of milk usually on the outside sill. Sometimes, Charlotte would see a hand grasp the bottle of milk and pull it inside, then replace it a few moments later.

Charlotte wrote short notes to me at college; her handwriting was barely readable. I recall her saying that the family across the hall cooked meat at all hours and that the smell had sealed itself forever into the woodwork and paint of the building.

So, for hours each evening Charlotte composed and rewrote her long, untitled poem about love. Lucy had said: "That's so *marvelous* that you can be so dedicated that way. I just know you're going to be a famous writer, Charlotte. You put everything into it."

On the advice of an older man friend, Lucy had begun carrying a small revolver in her purse.

One summer night Charlotte was feeling uneasy, restless. Love was too complex a subject. She had become lost in her long poem, and still was stuck about the title.

"Am I just lonely?" she asked herself. She put on her black coat and black beret and walked out into the deserted street which shone under orange street lamps, for a soft rain was falling. She turned a corner and saw a drunken couple arguing on a door stoop.

The woman was yelling at the man: "Don't *tell* me that! I've heard all of that before. You'll *never* change. You can't *fool* me. You're a pig, you make me so sick...."

The man said something then, too softly, low and pleading.

"Oh no you don't, buddy," the woman said. "I'll *never* trust you. I'll *never* believe anything *you* ever say to me again... disgusting pig."

Charlotte refused to hear more. As she crossed the street and passed quickly to another block, she heard a door slam.

She arrived finally at the tavern where Lucy Williams was a singer. The place was dark and Lucy was nowhere in sight. The strings of blue and red blinking fights around the low ceiling depressed Charlotte. She moved towards the bar counter, shaking rain from her beret. She asked the bartender when Gale would be performing, and was told ten o'clock.

Charlotte ordered a whiskey. She was chilled. She had never tasted whiskey and with her first sip thought, "Maybe I will learn something important from this drink."

A man was suddenly beside her, standing and leaning an elbow on the counter. He was short, balding, with a puffy, pink face. He wore thick eyeglasses and a red plaid wool scarf. "May I buy you that drink?"

"No," said Charlotte. "No, I don't think that would be good."

"I understand that. That's very wise."

"A dear friend of mine is a singer at this bar," Charlotte told the man.

"Are you an artist, then?"

"I'm a poet. I'm at work right now on a very long poem, in fact, but I got tired and came out for a drink, and to hear my friend sing." She finished her drink and the bartender poured her another.

"What is this poem about?" her new companion asked.

"Well, I don't have a title yet. So, I don't want to talk about it."

"Yes, yes, that's certainly a very good code to follow."

Charlotte says that she realised at that moment that her long poem about love was really more of a fable. Two black men hurried past the rain-soaked window. Charlotte thought, a fable about black men in love...but that is too complex; a poet's life is too complex and sad.

"It's certainly been a trying night for me," the man was saying, and a line of perspiration had formed on his forehead. "My mother's little poodle dog died. Oh, Mother was certainly devoted to that dog. She rescued it from death, you know. Abandoned at a roadside, and Mother saw it and scooped it up and raised it. Certainly loved that poodle. The dog became completely loyal, as pets will."

"Well, that was very gallant of your mother," Charlotte said. Gallant was the wrong word, Charlotte realised. And Charlotte says that was the instant she saw herself as a fraud: what rigid moral standards she held, and though she was quick to declare them, she did not actually live by.

"Yes. And Mother has had so many disappointments. She's certainly endured her share of heartache. Tables turning right and left, and people's vicious lies. Finally, it was this dog she loved better than anyone. And now it has died."

"That's terrible." Charlotte was sincere, but also irritated.

"When you've finished your drink, I'd be happy to walk you home. What is your name?"

Charlotte's need for secrecy formed a lie: she said her name was Lucy Gale. The man introduced himself as Dick. As a few uncertain jazzy notes were played on the piano and Charlotte's roommate Lucy appeared in her red dress on a little platform in the corner of the room, Charlotte and Dick left the tavern.

She was distracted as they walked the few blocks to her building. "I refuse to be jealous of women," she told herself. "Or of women who can sing in nightclubs."

The man chatted on about his mother's failing health, one of his neighbors who was robbed, a terrifying accident he'd had as a child. "I still have the scar!" He bought a bottle of inexpensive wine and they climbed the three short flights to Charlotte's apartment.

"We'll sit in there," Charlotte said, motioning him into Lucy's room. She did not want this man to see her writing, her bed, or the window with the milk bottle. She did not want him to see the box in which she kept ointment and dressings for her legs. She produced two water glasses from the bathroom and they sat on basket chairs and drank the wine.

"And so you study shorthand? That's certainly an excellent skill for a girl to have. I had a cousin who was very fast and efficient in her shorthand and typing. Now, this girl came down with a very rare and severe disease. Weakening of the arteries. Palpitations. Lost her mind altogether finally. We had her in a very fine place upstate. The poor thing did not even recognise me or Mother. We'd ask her questions and no matter what questions we'd ask, she'd always answer yes. Well, there are certainly worse ways to live, I suppose. Some people always answer no."

The poetic fable was forming itself: it would be about the awesome complexities and verities of love. Charlotte was frowning; she felt desperate suddenly to have this pitiful little man leave. People always tell such awful stories...

Dick eventually got to complaining that he felt ill. Charlotte loosened his red plaid wool scarf and placed a pillow behind him. "This happens sometimes," he explained. "I get ill with cramps. I perspire." He was pale, bits of his thin hair stuck to his temples.

And still Charlotte could not think of a title for her long fable-poem. Her visitor had fallen into a sound, noiseless sleep.

Charlotte took a newspaper which was several days old from a pile on the table and turned the first few pages. An entire page was devoted to the story of a teenage girl who had shot and killed her mother. It had happened just after breakfast. Apparently, the mother had scolded her about her clothing and poor grades. The account interviewed several neighbors, and one of the girl's school friends. The headline read TEEN GIRL KILLS MOM. It amused Charlotte to think that perhaps that would be the perfect title for her poetic fable about love.

She tried to awaken Dick; she read him the article and its headline. "Don't you think this is a scream?" she inquired of the bald, damp crown of his head, but he did not move or answer.

Charlotte was tired. That meaty smell in the building angered her. She folded a clean towel and placed it near her guest for the morning.

Dick was gone when Charlotte awoke, but he called at noon. "Lucy," he said, "I only wanted to say what a charming companion you were last night, what a wonderful time I had. I certainly was not at my best. I think it may have been food poisoning." He told Charlotte all that he had eaten the previous day and night. "But, I was thinking, wouldn't it be nice if I took you out for supper? Then maybe I could bring you over to meet Mother. Mother takes these new red pills, she's much better."

As Dick was speaking, Charlotte was thinking that there was probably something wrong with her mind. She had no desire to talk to anyone. She did not feel contempt, she explains, and she did not think it was fear. It was just that she did not want any interaction with people. Their lives, opinions, ideas, projects, their dreams, and the awful stories they told, were of no interest to her. Charlotte says that maybe she developed an allergy to other people's moods. Was there a medicine she could take? To loosen what she thought of as a tarnished lock in her mind, which had

26

captured all curiosity and empathy? She said to Dick: "I really am not up to making new friends right now."

"Well, that is certainly an admirable code to follow, Lucy."

"Yes," said Charlotte, "the more I think about it, the more I'm coming to believe that I really don't want much to do with people. That must be my...nature."

Dick told her about his grandfather with that exact same disorder, content only when reading and walking alone in the park. A very gruesome death, too: clunked on the head by a steel beam.

Charlotte did not speak to anyone for many more days, nor leave her room. When that fiery Lucy would stop home to change her dress and discuss her adventures, Charlotte pretended to be sleeping.

During this time there was little progress on the poem which was a fable. She wrote:

Forever winks at her

and was intrigued, but unable to continue.

Charlotte's sister Annie visited the cramped apartment soon after and was alarmed by that smell of cooking meat and Charlotte's state: unclean, malnourished, her sunken eyes, her dead tone and irrational words. "I think there are spies in this building," Charlotte declared, like she was telling a naughty joke.

Annie lived in a penthouse in the city, was married to Dr Rosenberg, and her daughter was only a few months old. Charlotte told her sister she wanted to go home, to the town where we all grew up. She mentioned me, also—that she was lonely without me. Annie could not fathom what Charlotte's experience on her own had meant or her condition, and surely could not predict its results.

"I was a failure there," Charlotte says now. "I was not meant for busy streets and all the sadness and meanness. I just wanted to come home."

I make an analysis of my friend based on this peculiar story, and it brings me usually to her fears. I know she used to race madly past houses with chimneys, frightened that they'd crumble and a brick would hit her. She has always been aware of the myriad fascinating ways people are killed or disfigured. She is reverent toward dwarves and giants, amputees, those with rare diseases or unusual handicaps— respectful, at least, at the idea of such people. It is that people are able to summon up courage and motivation to withstand so much, while Charlotte herself can only cope with these few rooms, the view from the windows, the sounds and stories of our little world, and me. Charlotte discovered this house, adored it immediately. Annie despised it, because it is so dilapidated and in the poorest section of the town, away from the shops and good houses. So, much against the counsel and wishes of Annie and Aunt Kaye, this house was purchased, and Charlotte settled in. She made it a nest, a place where she could see and hear all she would need to, that would admit no unpleasant stories. She'd found a place to be, forever.

Then, I had that trouble at school. My first plan was to move to the city myself, pursue my own writing—nothing so grand or painfull as a poetic fable about love, just my short stories, reviews, articles. I perceive Charlotte as having retreated from the world on account of fear; but, of course, I too have retreated. It is laziness, or timidity. I am a cautious person. Charlotte was overjoyed when I returned home and agreed to move in with her. It completed something for Charlotte, it sealed her safety. What did it do to me?

Well, I do not much like this town, but I enjoy our narrow back porch and taking my walks.

It strikes me every so often that there is nothing to wait for here. A storm may hit. The train stops, and then departs. But no miracle will come and give life to the motionless river. And all that is sad to me about our life here, or unsatisfying or bleak, is exactly what Charlotte loves.

Autumn

Four

There is an old grey stone convent, between our town and the next. Riding the train towards the city, you can catch a glimpse of its red tile roof and then, around the next bend, it is fully visible, ugly and ominous. There is a school, too, and all my life I have seen the youngsters in their uniforms—the boys wear white shirts, red ties, black pants and shoes; the girls wear navy blue skirts and vests over white blouses—carrying satchels, walking in twos and threes. It has always seemed to me those children were stronger, that their lives were more ordered and clear, somehow. I felt envy, wishing to join their club; I imagined they were better taken care of than I.

But Charlotte said those kids gave her the creeps; she scowled when she saw them. "They always do what they're told, and if they disobey, a nun will hit them," Charlotte declared.

I must have been eight or nine years old when I asked my father if I could go to that convent school. He laughed and said: "Oh, no. You have to be Catholic to go there, and we're not Catholic."

I asked: "What are we, then?"

We were in my father's study, lined floor to ceiling with crammed bookshelves, decorated with framed maps, busts of dead presidents, and he sat in his big green leather chair with a legal pad on his lap, an open briefcase on the floor beside him. He looked at me. "Well," said he casually and dismissively, "actually, we're nothing."

▼

Charlotte's new project the last week or so has been to write a story. She has several times begun working; I have seen her biting a pencil, scowling as she considers which word to use, how to structure a sentence. This enterprise, she says, is inspired by me. "The short story is such an exquisite, controlled form, such a perfect form." She has asked for my

31

help. I'm trying to put her off; I've been discouraged and distracted lately, waiting for word from my publisher.

I walked down the hill this morning to the post office. Humid and still and too bright. It does not seem a good sign that I have headaches so early in the day.

Mrs Turner was at the post office when I arrived. There was barely space for both of us to stand in that tiny room. She rested a paper sack of groceries on her hip. Peg Pelliteer did not even glance at me; she blew cigarette smoke in a harsh cone shape out of the side of her mouth and with her ring finger patted the stiff waves in her hair. "When Howard was alive, well, we would go down see a show and have supper some nice place. That was lovely. This was before the plays were all about naked people and Negroes. Plays used to be real fun, uplifting. We liked the musicals. I loved *My Fair Lady*. You know, that was a beautiful show. Now it's all about Negroes and naked people writhing around. No use for the city."

"Oh, I know, I know," Mrs Turner said. She looked at me, smiled weakly, embarrassed, and stepped back a bit, to make room for me.

But Peg Pelliteer continued. 'You take your life in your hands down there. The crime. And bums sleeping on the street corner, sometimes you think they're lying there dead. People just step right over them."

"We don't have money for weekends in the city," said Mrs Turner, miserably.

"Well, I'll say you're not missing much. It isn't any more like when we were girls and you'd get on a lovely evening gown, a strapless evening gown, and the shoes matched the bag, and you'd go for a date with some nice, polite young man and you would have supper in one of the restaurants at one of the big hotels. Then dancing. I'm talking about during the war, you know."

What a ridiculous old bird, I was thinking as I feigned patience and examined the posted signs addressing philatelic concerns. How appalling, the way people will weave myths about those old, better days. Peg Pelliteer was probably just an unhappy horse-faced girl, abandoned in some hotel lobby with matching bag and shoes.

"Now, every old, beautiful place has been all torn down. Negroes, foreigners all over. The girls get pregnant at thirteen years old, and they all take drugs, and sometimes you think these people would as soon stab out your guts for a five dollar bill as look at you."

Stab out your guts for a *quarter,* I was thinking.

"It isn't even civilized anymore," said Peg Pelliteer.

"Oh, I know," agreed Mrs Turner.

"It used to be such a civilized place." She looked at me, then. She stepped away from her wire-covered window and returned after a second. "Just some bills. Nothing from those publisher people, yet."

I thanked her, I nodded to Mrs Turner. Walking up the hill towards our house, fuming, I went over as I have before, what I should have said to Peg Pelliteer—about minding her own business, not scrutinizing our mail or announcing its contents, about just doing her wretched little job.

Charlotte is never interested in the mail, but when I mentioned that Peg Pelliteer the post-mistress had been monologuing again, Charlotte said: "Tell me. Tell me everything."

▼

I've been commissioned to write a review of a new novel. I had forgotten the title, but knew the author's last name is Brooks or Brooking or something. A *wunderkind,* the current genius, the new literary voice. In the city this morning, I popped into Buckeye, my favorite book store.

In the True Crime section, I backed into someone, excused myself, and saw it was an acquaintance. "Hi, Willie," I said.

He said: "It's Terry."

Dampened and embarrassed, I said: "Oh yes, Terry... right," and frowned, scrutinizing the faded spines of books.

"So, how are things going?" I asked, but this casual friendliness was stiff. It's rare that I'm friendly. Friendly only when all things are right and aligned, the weather is perfect and nothing hurts. My ordinary question was a little frantic, also, for how things were going for Terry was sadly apparent: he was supporting himself with a cane, was rail thin and his face was covered with red blotches. His eyes were huge, sunken, his cheekbones protruded.

"Not too well," said Terry bluntly.

My expression scrunched with a concerned look—eyebrows up,

thin smile—some expression I've learned from movies. But it was not ingenuine, not phony; just pressured and tense and awkward.

Terry described his current condition, some infection I hadn't heard of before, which weakens the legs. "This AIDS," he said, "it just confuses everyone, even the doctors."

And where did I know him from? He used to be cute, I think. A real flirt with long hair, sort of obnoxious.

He is living at a hotel downtown now, he was saying, and getting money from Social Security, and he quoted his blood counts, numbers of cells, some which dropped, some which rose, and he looked at me, wryness edging out that defeated sense beneath the surface.

Smarting still over my blunder about his name, I wanted to say how he looked exactly like someone I know named Willie, but it seemed a weak explanation.

"So, anyway, I just keep hanging in there," he said. "I'm in room 207. Ever want to come visit, it's room 207." Terry pulled an old British mystery from the shelf and plodded slowly along the aisle to the front counter.

▼

In the late afternoon of this bruised, breathless day, I found myself further downtown, just near the porno place.

I stood outside for a few moments, gazing absently at the photos in the window, peeking through the door, casual.

A bus honked, a man down the street was yelling at a vendor. I pushed through the door—glass painted black— and there was a familiar jingle sound.

An old man with crossed eyes and a white beard was seated behind a counter. I handed him two dollar bills and he gave me a stack of gold tokens. I nodded to him. I cupped the tokens in my hand, rattled them, smoothed them with my thumb.

The front room, where the merchandise is on display, is brightly lit by buzzing florescent tubes overhead. Metal racks and glass cases exhibit dildos of every shape and color, huge ones with thick veins, monster dicks wrapped in cellophane. There is a variety of lubrication, condoms, oils and instruments, rubber, whips, handcuffs. This sort of paraphernalia doesn't interest me much; I'm too conventional and old-fashioned, I guess.

Then, along the walls are the magazines, in separate sections: regular straight porn, gay male porn, lesbian porn, transvestites, bondage, S/M, erotica, fetish. Here, too, I show myself as rather pedestrian, passing directly to the rack of magazines for gay men, absorbing the familiar, now hardly tantalizing images of sneering blond boys holding enormous erect dicks, muscles, posing, and the bright, colorful lettering of the great code words: HEAT, STROKE, CADET, THRUST, BOY, HARD, MAN, LUST, SAILOR, SUCK, BLOW, CUM.

At the back of the place is a doorway, covered by a curtain and surrounded by a string of red, blinking Christmas lights. I stepped through, into the maze. It is a large room, divided by movie booths which are constructed of cheap wood and crooked doors with simple hinges and handles; above each door are signs—VACANT and IN USE—respectively lit blue or red.

At first it's pitch black. Then, someone flares a match to light a cigarette, illuminating posters of naked men and those ominous, farfetched signs—ONLY ONE PERSON ALLOWED PER BOOTH. They play a popular radio station, songs I don't know. It takes a few moments for my eyes to get adjusted.

The ceiling is low. Bulbs are embedded in the ceiling but they do not really illuminate, they do not cast true shadows; they glow and beam, coloring the room dull orange. Under that light, the men's faces are pretty bronze, one cannot see the blemishes and lines. But, too, everyone seems like he's wearing a wig. Hair seems shiny and fake.

It's almost like candlelight, this light.

As I always do, I moved to a corner between two booths, vacant just then, a place from which the view is most inclusive; I leaned back against the wall, my ankles crossed, one knee bent, hands in pockets. This is my pose, nothing very studied or inviting.

There are eight or ten men wandering around. Crowded for so early on such a sunny afternoon. Some lean against walls, some keep roaming.

I take inventory of the place. I give the men names. Billy is tall, clean, filled out, he strolls confidently and unsubtly looks over each man he passes.

Dennis, probably on his lunch hour, is wearing an expensive tailored suit and red tie. He walks briskly, shoes clicking, businesslike, exactly as he must walk through the office where he works.

Sal is short and tight: tight jeans, tight shirt, piercing pointy boots and slick tight hair and mustache, lots of tight muscles. He can hardly walk, he waddles, and his head moves, like a mechanical thing, right and left, scrutinizing, relentlessly arrogant. He looked me up and down, stared at my crotch, swaggered along the maze.

There's one so tall he has to duck to enter through the curtain. I've seen him before and named him Connie. Slow moving, very thin, styled, blond-colored hair. His collar is up, tassels on the shoes, and his big, round eyes gaze down wearily at the slim potential in the room. He stops at a booth, stands in its open doorway; he lights a cigarette and exhales a long, sharp cylinder of smoke above all our heads.

There are a few I just call Mister; these are older men, bespectacled, well-dressed; they look like they're shopping for sport shirts, they're furtive, they're lonely I reckon.

And, then, several I think of as kids; with crazy hair, leather jackets, ripped jeans, cute butts; this activity for young boys is only a lark, capricious. It means nothing to them.

What does it mean to me?

My heart beats fast, like I've taken some drug, which must be what I like about the place. But I am amused, too, watching the other men. Heads don't move, only the eyes. Everyone appears disinterested, almost serene. It's phony, of course. All of their hearts are going, too.

The static, tinny piped-in music and shuffling, shuffling. Then, I look around and one of them is missing—Dennis or Sal or one of the Misters—and off to the side, in the orange dimness, a door is closing softly. Contact.

My own requirements for contact are many. This kind of casual sex is for me not at all casual. So much goes into finding the right man. There is the look, of course; but that is not so simple as mere size or hair color. The shape of a jaw, the walk, the profile. Eyebrows are important. The expression matters, too; so many of these men have a turn at the corners of the mouth that signals desperation, pleading, some kind of ultimate importance to all of this. This attitude puts me off. I like to be able at least to imagine a man having a life outside of these cubicles, away from the codified postures and the droning blue light of porno movies.

I need sexy, strong, handsome, someone unpredictable; it's the eyes really; I like amused, intelligent, kind eyes. As a youngster, in such places, in the context of temporary love, I was invulnerable and could take on any type of man. I enjoyed flaming contempt, something quick. These encounters only existed to be added to my history, I didn't feel them, I didn't care. Now, though, even here, I need kindness.

A handsome, slender, black man, walked in with his hands in his pockets and made a quick tour of the place. He settled against the wall opposite me. He kept his head down. His hair was black, wavy. He was wearing tan slacks and a black jacket. It was so dark, it was hard to know if he was looking at me or not. Then he opened the door to a booth, backed in, left the door open. I waited a second, followed him. This silent etiquette, arranged so many years ago by unknown, unsung choreographers, sometimes works just perfectly.

He closed and latched the door behind me, plunked one of his tokens in the little slot and the movie came on. We grabbed each other's crotches, kneading. It was silly, I was already bored. We took our jackets off and dropped them on the small bench. In less than a minute, the movie flickered off, and I put in one of my tokens.

In the quick, dusty beam of the ancient projector, which barely lit our tiny, dark space, I saw this man's eyes, dark and wide and sloping, and his smooth brown cheeks and throat. I put my hand on the back of his head, stroked his hair, his neck.

We undid each other's pants. His fell to his knees and the belt clunked. He reached for me. At first we held each other's dicks, squeezing, pulling.

Sometimes it is like the penis is an object between men, a thing to attend to, which keeps us from the vagueness or risk of desire. But I don't go there merely for penises; I go to touch. I stepped closer, pushed against him in an embrace, which he resisted, and then accepted. We held each other. That's what I like.

We went on this way for some time. I passed my hand over all of his body, between and under his legs. I touched his hard dick—it curved slightly to the right—and then held his face in my palms, and we kissed a little.

Finally, he started jerking himself off, staring at me, breathing hard. He said: "I'm close." His voice was high and soft. When he came on the floor, he grabbed my shirt sleeve tight with his fingers. I watched the top of his head, a shiny brown scalp through black curls.

I came too, splattering on the wall. By this time, the movie had stopped again, the booth was very dark. We pulled up our pants, tucked in shirts. I handed him his jacket and took my own.

This arena—for whatever else it may give me or take away—is distinctly mine. It is comfortable. Here, I can observe and know some touches of seduction, desire, diplomacy, privacy. An hour or so among these strangers tells me so much more about myself than I am able to learn at home. Home is a constant contest, a loving battle with Charlotte; it is the daily walks through the poor, unchanging streets of our town.

Charlotte's thoughtful analysis is that coming to the porno place allows me to play out the role of bad boy, to be naughty and secretive. I will seek danger, but not intimacy. It is an old topic for Charlotte and me, part of a larger discourse on love and closeness. She says I think with my dick.

After the cramped sex, standing in the booth, elbows hitting the walls, after it is over I always have a flash of a wish to get a good look at my man, to see him in the open; but I always head straight out, back into daylight, and I keep walking, I do not look back.

I had to race to make the train home. I ran and sucked in deep breaths, pounding my feet against the city sidewalk hard, in an effort to feel fit.

▼

Henry Beale was not a writer, and he did not like to read. He could not help telling lies, and was addicted to crises.

Our first summer together, we were just twenty. I had met Henry one night in the city. He was wearing one long feather earring and black eyeliner. Sitting on a parked car in front of a bar, just before closing, he was doing Thelma Ritter from *All About Eve,* and his friends were hooting, clapping.

38

It was dawn and Henry Beale and I went to a diner for French toast. Henry told me how really unhappy he was. He was full of complaints about the city: the heat and violence and crowds. He had been taking too many drugs. He had just been dumped by his lover, Chris, an ex-priest. We took a cab to a shitty little room Henry was renting. Daylight poured through white pillowcases he'd hung over the windows, and we listened to Duke Ellington records. I was sick from the beer and the night, but still there was a romantic, sweet feeling which I have always remembered. Anguished, crying, Henry asked if he could come stay with me for a day or two. He was with us all summer.

I was fully occupied with a novella I was writing, a preposterous, stylish little thing, full of references. Charlotte said it was brilliant. Henry was just in my way and my irritation grew meatier and more profound.

"You're like some guy from another century or something," he said to me. He was pulling potato chips from a bag and popping them in his mouth with one hand, flipping the dial on the television with the other. I knew I could not love Henry Beale.

Henry and Charlotte, though, got along like comfortable old companion cats. This was the marijuana summer— someone had given me a pot plant and Charlotte had heard how to pick off the leaves and cure them in the oven. So, she and Henry would get stoned all morning, watch the game shows and giggle, mess up the kitchen with their frantic inventions (bananas and sugar and jam and chocolate), and then they'd sleep off their terrific headaches in chairs on the back porch, and I would have some peace.

Evenings, in the kitchen, the windows wide open, drawing in the still air and moths, they'd get drunk on wine and laugh loud. I remember forcefully closing my bedroom door to convey the message that their fun was interfering with my work.

At night: "We're going swimming," and they would clutch at each other, snorting laughter, slapping the screen door behind them. I could hear them race down the gravel of Station Road. I knew they were stripping off their clothes, leaping naked over the rocks into that shallow, cold spot of the river where it is safe to swim. Hearing them return, shouting whispers at each other, I wondered; And what am I doing up here, dry? Am I such a serious person that I cannot get drunk and strip

39

and swim?

I felt such furious jealousy at being excluded from their adventures. And a sadness at my distance from what I saw as freedom shared by my forever friend, Charlotte, and my boyfriend, Henry Beale. Like the sadness when you pass a restaurant and at a table right in the window is a group of clean, cheery people, just relaxed and full, rich, colored by belonging, and they're laughing, laughing, and you wonder: What can they be laughing at?

Henry and Charlotte formed a quick, sure bond. But, what was it they talked about until sunrise? I know that Henry believed in God. Charlotte had nothing to say about God, only the perfect process of evolution. Dialogues about organized religion and man controlling nature. Sluggish, loud voices, repetition. Henry's position was Communist, really, though he was too naive to have called it that. Charlotte espoused the social, aesthetic advantages of the old monarchies, favoring an ordered society where everyone knew their place. And I remember one heated debate about public schools versus private schools, and quite a few others about art. Finally, their glassy eyes would turn to me, standing grumpy in a corner with my cup of coffee, for an educated opinion on whatever was the topic.

It was hot. The windows and doors were all open. Charlotte took a huge swallow of her insanely strong coffee and insisted: "Ontogeny recapitulates philogeny." And Henry Beale mused for some seconds and then wondered: "What do you mean by 'recapitulates'?"

They were having fun, they were finding profundity; and I fumed. Charlotte seemed to me so petty and contrived that summer. She flirted obviously, but safely, with the lover I did not even love.

In bed, Henry told me: "I'm happy." The room was blue-black dark, the radio turned to a talk program, too low to hear any words, only the changes in tone. Three of Henry's bony fingers lightly pressed against my throat, my cheek. He kissed me. Always he would kiss my neck, then my shoulder; and his giant hands would pass over my body, down to my butt, around to my prick. I responded to Henry Beale, following a lead.

Henry smiled, drew on his cigarette, swirled it in the air above us so its orange end made fast, crazy shapes. "I'm happy," Henry said.

I began to cry.

He was up on his elbow, then, holding onto my shoulder, saying my name. "What is it? What *is* it?"

I could not talk to Henry Beale. The answer: that I was not happy, that I did not know what this splendid, funny man even meant by the word.

▼

It has been quite a few years since Charlotte has gone for any naked dunks in the river. Tonight, with a short, thick pencil Charlotte writes a sentence, crosses it out, writes it again, changing a word or tense. And crosses it out again, vigorously. She has a few pages laid out on her bed, organized by some code of her own.

"I have the people in my mind," she told me. "They're in my mind, and they say things. They have conversations with each other. And I know them, I know them. But can't seem to form the words, to write them down. I know what they look like. And I know their moods. I have this one man— most of my people are men—and he is very fat, but tall, and does not dress in very neat clothes, and he has this tiny dog who is old and practically crippled, and the man is very content. He's serene. But tall and very fat, just huge, almost a monster. But polite. That's the thing about this giant man: he is very polite." Charlotte has this expectant expression on her face: see, I made up a story!

I do adore Charlotte. She is earnest, and not many people are. She will not venture out or forward, has designed her life to stay protected from unpleasantness and searching, and is free, then, to tap into her delicious dreams.

I remember when we were very small children and our families held a picnic in our backyard. Our mothers set the table, and the napkins kept flying away; the mothers were furious, but I laughed. My father was red-faced, trying to get the charcoal going with kerosene, staring at the coals, passing his hand over them, dejected at his lack of expertise. Charlotte's father was extremely tall and slouched, and I recall him in a filthy apron, turning hamburgers on the grill.

Charlotte sat off by herself, in a spot of shade. Annie tried to coax her to come and sing songs; her mother implored her to help; but Charlotte

41

would not budge. She rested her chin on her skinned, bony knees, which she hugged like a best doll. I skipped over to her, stared for a moment. "What are you doing, Charlotte?"

"Just wondering," Charlotte said.

Even as a little boy, I knew, deep inside, what a splendid thing that was to say. And still this memory is an unhappy one, as childhood memories finally are for me; it dissolves in a kerosene wash.

▼

Still no word from XXX Press, Inc. It might just as well be rejection. I don't think this novel of mine is any great masterpiece or anything. I really feel very humble about it. I have no reason to expect that it will be published; but, still, rejection sinks me into a familiar, floating sense that I am unloved, not good enough.

That meddlesome Peg Pelliteer, noting as she always does that I've had no reply from the publisher, asked: "Hey, what is your book about, anyways?"

"Illness," I said.

Five

Aunt Kaye was here this morning, whispering sternly to Charlotte. I know what it's all about, have known for some time. Aunt Kaye feels, rightly enough, that I should regularly be paying rent. I am not able to contribute any money to our household now; Charlotte and I both understand it's out of the question. Aunt Kaye, of course, believes that unless I can make an arrangement to pay rent and share expenses, I should not be living here. The severe set of her shoulders and tightness of her lips indicate that Aunt Kaye is taking a stand, but she is no challenge to Charlotte. Charlotte is pure loyalty. It is irrelevant to her whether I have money or not, and when funds do appear in my life, as they do from time to time, she never makes any requests. Whatever guilt feelings I may have had regarding finances have long since been defused.

Their discussion is polite and subdued, as always, and ends with Aunt Kaye saying: "I hope you know my position has nothing to do with the young man himself. He's very charming, I'm sure."

I don't feel very charming, actually.

"I just think it is my duty to make recommendations in your best interests."

Charlotte comforted Aunt Kaye, let her off the hook, ushered her out the door, and then we got ready for breakast.

"I'm tired of eggs," I said. "And now they say they're not even good for you."

"We could make some toast, that's an easy thing to make," Charlotte offered. We were silent, then.

I am tormented by the process of feeding myself, by the choices involved and the necessity. Charlotte has learned to ignore it all, she does not even feel hunger. She likes grape juice, crackers, cocoa. She'll take a bite of an apple or a piece of a chocolate bar occasionally. She is drinking alcohol more and more lately, and earlier in the day. But, even as she gets skinnier, she worries about me and, in her fashion, urges me to take better care of myself.

These pouting, empty periods of mine affect writing as well as eating. I know it's an old story: the writer and his blank, accusing page. So many take alcohol or drugs to fuel themselves, but for me that is a worthless option. I only get stiff and my head aches and for days I seem not to care if I ever write again.

Very often, in fact, I do not care about ever writing again, except that it is who I am. When I was eleven, I was inspired deeply and mysteriously by *The Hardy Boys* series, written by Franklin W. Dixon. We owned the first edition volumes; they had been my father's. On the brown cardboard cover was a silhouette of the two male figures, crouching, inspecting something with a magnifying glass. Frank and Joe Hardy, teenagers, drove a roadster and acted like grownups. They had, it seemed to me, unique access to the adult world, were allowed entrance to any place their investigation took them. They had cleanliness and manners. They had purpose, moral certainty. And, of course, they had each other.

So, at eleven, I wrote my first fiction. I used Mother's college Remington. The finished product was a pure, unapologetic imitation of the Hardy brothers, and weakly constructed, a seriously flawed mystery story of twenty or thirty pages. It was entitled *The Secret*. Back with that first effort, I exhibited the same weaknesses and strengths as I do now: no full sense of or interest in plot but some facility for dialogue, for character. I cared about my boys, and so they lived.

Mother said how wonderful my story was, just marvelous. My father read it all in one sitting, while I sat on the floor beside his chair. He corrected some of the spelling, had a suggestion or two, and gazed at me finally with the warmest, queerest smile, which I immediately knew meant that he liked me. He liked my story; but he liked more that I had written it, that I wanted someday to be a writer. He appreciated, I think, information that came not from the juvenile try at fiction itself, but from inside of me. He said: "This shows some real talent, son. Keep writing." It must be a wonderful thing to see your child's ambition.

Next, for a class I wrote a short story about a woman with no arms or legs, a circus performer who lit cigarettes using her lips and tongue. In the end, she hangs herself. Quite a feat!

The teacher—Charlotte reminded me her name was Miss Flume—had orange hair and a red face. He favorite book was *Huckleberry Finn*. When one asked: "Can I please go to the drinking fountain?" Miss Flume, of course, answered: "I don't know. Are you able?" And one would amend: "*May* I please go to the drinking fountain?" Then she'd refuse.

I showed my short story to Charlotte, who took in a deep breath and declared: "Oh, I *do* understand it."

Miss Flume read it aloud to the class, and they snickered. Miss Flume glared at me censoriously, but nevertheless said: "Well, class, it looks as though one of our students may just grow up to be a writer."

As for *The Secret*—a couple of years ago I found it stored in a box and Charlotte and I had great fun turning my brother sleuths into insanely sex-obsessed adolescents infiltrating a gay porn ring, sleeping with policemen, priests, criminals, and each other.

▼

The city library is a cavern made of marble floors and carved wood ceilings; the walls are stunning, curved leaded windows. In the center is a rotunda covered by a glass dome; the names of American authors are etched in stone beneath it. Twain. Melville. Hawthorne. Irving. James.

Two white-haired women sit idly at the little information desk, but smile eagerly at the people who pass. Everything about the library is old-fashioned. The card catalogue is dull teak, the drawers have tarnished brass handles.

I feel secure there, assured. I told Charlotte all I really want—as far as being a writer, that is—is to someday have a book of mine in that library. And then I can die happy, I said. Charlotte dismissed my modest goal and morbid reasoning: "Oh, you're not going to die. Stop saying you're going to die."

I enter in the early afternoon and sometimes do not get out until the sky is streaked with rose and grey at sunset. Loaded down with the biographies Charlotte asks me to check out, and a murder mystery or two for me, I'm painfully hungry, realizing I've eaten nothing all day. And what have I been up to in the library for these hours? Some kind of fantasy, some dream; like a dream, poorly recalled. I read back issues of newspapers. I browse through the antiquated short story collections, the history books. Something pricks my curiosity; I am led to one stack, then another, up and down the narrow iron staircases to obscure sections which I know so well. Then I am hard-pressed to think of what I've gained, what information or ideas I have absorbed, but I have been so busy, practically frantic in my search, and my pockets are full of scraps of paper with catalogue numbers.

The main reading room has reference books along the walls and three rows of heavy oak tables; at the tables are those wonderful old-fashioned lamps with green glass shades.

Today I invaded the cinema section, capturing the largest volumes with the most photographs. I went to one of the tables and sat at the end, far from a crumpled, cranky old man scribbling in a tablet. To ramble through Hollywood.

I love the movies from before I was born. Sepia-washed enormous smiles and the looks, the postures. I can stare forever at a still of carefree dancing partners, or one of a brave dying soldier with a bandage on his head being tended by a pretty nurse. And the fake cowboys before fake deserts, the fake families at their fake breakfasts.

Clifton Webb. Myrna Loy. Eleanor Powell. Alan Ladd. Miriam Hopkins. Margaret O'Brien. Brian Aherne.

Men with guns. Women in that fearful pose, knuckles to their lips, leaning back.

A giant, shiny black piano, surrounded by chorus girls dressed in tons of white tulle and—what are those costumes? Fruit bowls on their heads? That this artifice has meant so much to our world astonishes me.

I was tenderly turning pages, like I do with favorite poems, like people do with the *Bible*. Barbara Stanwyck and Fred MacMurray leering at each other, nasty and cold. Frances Farmer. Henry Beale used to put his fingers to his chest, look away and sigh: "It wasn't right what they did to her. Saint Frances."

Someone was suddenly near me, too close. It was my romance: Jesse. I've thought of this young man as a hero, or an object of desire, as a character in a book I'll write some day. But, romance is really the best, truest word. Jesse is a name I made up for him.

His straw-colored hair juts over his ears, brushes his collar. His eyes are green, his complexion sun-burnt and he needs a shave. He usually wears a plain grey or brown sweater and sneakers. He wears loose-fitting trousers without underwear, and my gaze is always drawn to his crotch. If his hair were combed and he were put into some clean, nice clothes, he'd be a handsome boy; and it is this very carelessness which attracts me. Beneath the layers of clothing it's clear his body is slender, firm, quick.

I've seen him here for weeks. We pass in an aisle, we're near each other in the fine, we're facing each other at the card catalogue, and Jesse looks directly into my eyes and he smiles. Warm, unchallenging, soft. But I look away. There is a subtle competition (in my mind, anyway): Jesse is forthright and friendly, engaging, sweet, and I am none of those things.

I have imagined encounters, eyes locking, subtle but revealing dialogues, and all that we may have in common. We'll go for coffee. There will be tense, scary chemistry. And I'll tell Charlotte all about it, of course.

Before today, he has never sat at my table. When he placed his pile of books down, my shoulders stiffened and I stared harder at the print on the page before me and a photograph of Dirk Bogarde grinning.

Moments passed, and I took a quick look at the bindings of his books. They were all astronomy texts. One was open to an illustration of the solar system, orange and silver circles against black. A glance at Jesse then: he had put on a pair of round glasses, he tapped a pencil against his notebook. He ran his fingers through his hair to push it back, but it fell again into his eyes. Romance.

Abruptly, Jesse turned a page and began underlining a paragraph. I must have moved in my seat, reacting. Jesse looked at me. His lively green eyes met my own weak brown ones. I was caught.

"I know," he said in a library-whisper. "It's bad. I shouldn't mark up the books."

"You could maybe Xerox the page," I said, and it sounded so idiotic.

"Yes, you're right. I'm a lazy shit." He returned his attention to the book then, away from me, and I felt the strangest sense of abandonment— this small interaction extended itself until I was convinced Jesse did not like me, had judged me, found me to be a bore.

A pouting Gloria Grahame stared up at me, but I'd completely lost interest, like a valve had been shut off.

Jesse shut his book and spoke to me: "We see each other here all the time, don't we?"

"Yes. You run into the same people if you come a lot." Which sounded weak and unthoughtful.

"Are you a student?"

"No. I'm a writer."

"No kidding? What? Novels?"

Breathlessly, too fast, I answered: "A lot of short stories and things, articles and things. I just finished a novel, and I'm sort of peddling it around to get it published."

Jesse slid across two chairs. He was next to me.

I asked: "You're a student?"

"I am definitely a student. But, not for long. I mean, I hate school, I hate the teachers and other students. I'm through with all of it."

"I see you're reading about astronomy. For a class?"

"No, this is for me. And it's bigger than just astronomy, or just what's in these books. Bigger than the facts about planets and stars. It's the concepts, the meaning of it. I'm so fascinated by circles, by motion, the way things work. I can't describe it, but that's why I'm reading through all this astronomy stuff."

I wanted to say I understood what he meant, but knew how solicitous I would sound. It's practically impossible to converse with handsome men.

We asked each other questions: Where do you live? Do you work? Do you like this or that author, this or that movie? Finally we asked each other's names; I said mine, he said: "Jesse."

He kept smiling, as though it were the easiest, most natural expression for him, and that was disconcerting. My smiles come out like frowns, I think.

Once in a while as we spoke his gaze would wander and I'd look at his pretty hair, his dark, strong arms. He had rather large ears, they stuck out. I liked that.

I liked Jesse. And then suddenly, he stood and gathered up his books. He looked down at me. "God, it's so late, I've got to go. See you again soon?"

I was startled. I nodded. I checked out a British spy novel for myself

48

and Strachey's *Queen Victoria* for Charlotte. I waited ten minutes, to be sure Jesse had left the building, then stepped out the side door for a smoke. There is a little playground attached to the parking lot. It is nothing more than adequate for children: cement blocks decorated with red, purple and green letters and numbers, and cartoon dogs painted on the gate. Swings, sand (it resembles dirt), and other useless stuff, surrounded by a patch of grass. Empty today. Too cold.

I stepped behind a wooden fence and was completely concealed between it and the building. Holding my books in one arm against my chest, I felt through my cotton trousers with my other hand, stroked lightly with two fingers. I was immediately hard.

Some voices. I froze. They passed.

Something had me determined to complete this, compelled to follow through. I unzipped my fly.

It's so rare for my dick to feel the cold of day, so rare for me to see it in such brightness. That alone was exciting, a strange freedom. I pounded away fast and in a minute felt that most ancient, most familiar feeling at the back of my knees, and then, just as one of my books fell, I spurted all over some wet leaves.

I raced for the train and rode the whole way home tapping my fingers against my knee. Funny, I had arbitrarily picked the name Jesse for my library romance, and it turns out it is his true name. (I know Charlotte so well: she will read that coincidence as a sign. Maybe I should not tell her about Jesse.)

The train passed the Oasis Motel with the green neon palm tree on the roof, my landmark indicating I'm half-way home, and I realised I'd forgotten to go for my blood tests in the city. I will go tomorrow.

▼

Tonight was the first frost. I made a pot of hot chocolate and lit a fire in the fireplace, and we sat on the rug. Charlotte took one sip of brandy and pretended to be drunk, giggled at nothing, could not get her sentences out.

That old, cracked mirror with the ornate, gold-colored frame was leaning against the wall—we never can decide where to hang it. How

I hate mirrors. I have spent all my life lowering my head when I come near a mirror and breezing past shop window reflections. I could see our movement in the glass, bathed in dull orange from the fire light. I was remembering the time in Charlotte's life she calls her "sassy days." The summer we were sixteen, when she was considered eccentric, maybe even a little dangerous, and she loved the persona.

She strolled with infinite assurance down the sloping main street of our town, wearing a black dress that came to below her knee and a black shirt pinned with a rhinestone at the collar. Enormous dark glasses practically covered her face, leaving visible only white cheeks with crude dabs of rouge. She had cut her black hair short, and a bit lopsided. She would sit alone on the stone bench at the town square, her long legs spread apart; she smoked cigarettes and tossed the butt-ends, stained with a hideous crimson lipstick onto the grass. Her very posture signalled a fast, firm departure from custom.

I remember the boys laughed at her. They drove past in their cars, tooted the horn, shouted and sped away, coating Charlotte's shoes with pebbles and dust. And when Charlotte stopped into Hornstein's store to buy a magazine, the girls who gathered there looking at cosmetics and drinking sodas would whisper; they would watch Charlotte's easy, independent gait as she left, and smooth out their own pretty dresses, touch their own soft and styled hair in an absent way, sadly, as though they feared this creature in black might somehow have spoiled their studied loveliness.

She had little time for me that summer. I missed and envied her. She had cultivated a new, private defense, it seemed to me, found some better road, and left me alone to endure as best I could. She wouldn't play cards, and had outgrown our seances in which we tried to contact certain famous criminals and actresses. I was reading *Madame Bovary* and had no one with whom to discuss it.

She'd taken up with a puffy younger girl named Jeanne, a premature sex kitten, full of stories. Jeanne was enamored of Charlotte. It became a usual sight that summer: Charlotte in black, moving with long, confident strides through the dusty side streets of the town, down to the river or to the train station or towards the woods, and that obnoxious Jeanne following her, eager to keep pace. They smoked cigarettes and Jeanne coughed. Jeanne told ridiculous tales about rendezvous with sailors in the city. And I think Charlotte really did not pay much attention to her new friend; when they were together, Charlotte seemed condescending, dismissive. I do not know why Charlotte abandoned me for Jeanne that summer. I mourned our togetherness. I cried, I think.

The alliance was ended by Jeanne's mother who telephoned Charlotte's father to say she had learned some things about Charlotte, disagreeable, objectionable things— that Charlotte swam naked at the reservoir (which everyone did), that she stayed out of doors too late at night, and all the cigarette smoking. Charlotte was not a nice companion or a good influence for her daughter, Jeanne's mother insisted in a high-pitched voice, her tone angry and defensive. Charlotte's father only said yes, of course, that he was sorry she felt that way. By then, I suppose, Charlotte's father was just a very tired man.

Charlotte never again spoke a word to Jeanne or gave her even the briefest glance. Very soon, Charlotte and I were back together, with a new passion: listening to opera records, which we found hilarious. At the end of August, we had our picnic and Charlotte got her burns.

Tonight, for one moment, that old mirror described a young Charlotte, her blunt smile defying pain, white skin and that crazy hair. And I was reflected too: off to the side, sad-eyed, watching her, watching her. In that light, in the distortion of the cracked glass and memory, the planes of my face, framed by close-cut hair, the angle of my jaw, my huge, worried eyes showed a boy just waiting to be a handsome, good man.

"Don't you think there should be special laws about that?" Charlotte was saying.

"What's that? I don't know."

"What I've been trying to explain to you." She lit a cigarette and shook the match vigorously. "If a woman kills her husband, because she really, really can't stand him, right? And she goes to trial and they find her guilty. All right, fine. But, why should she have to go to jail? I mean, she's not a threat to society or anything. She only killed her husband because she hated him, and she wouldn't do it again. And they could make a law that she is not allowed to get remarried."

Can I tell Charlotte when my head is pounding? It will scare her, perhaps. She monitors my symptoms in order to dismiss them. She will

51

not acknowledge disease—too complicated, because acknowledging disease means allowing for doctors and hospitals and medication, for progression, and then death. Too complicated.

But, are my headaches, I wonder, brought on by disease? Maybe they're brought on, at least some of the time, by Charlotte.

Six

"Keep your head up," Charlotte said. "Now, turn a tiny bit. That's good."

Annie leaned against the window frame, her arms crossed. A pale blue sweater was pulled over her shoulders. She drew deeply on a cigarette and exhaled. She was watching several of the Turner children in the road, engaged in some violent and unfair child sport, their ages and genders indiscernible, only small figures in worn coats and hats. "How many children does that woman have, anyway?" Annie said impatiently.

"Don't move the angle of your chin," said Charlotte from her bed. "I'm doing your profile right now, so keep still. And why is your hair up that way? That beautiful hair, all knotted up. Take it down, Annie, please."

Annie reached around and took out three pins, her hair fell to her shoulders. She tapped ash from her cigarette onto the window sill. She is now, as she always has been, a magnificent figure, strong and graceful. Generations of women's faces combine to form hers; keen bitter and joyous memories carve the tiny lines, set the shoulders. She's here for a visit. Her divorce from Dr Rosenberg was final last week; an eleven year marriage is over. And despite it, this time in Annie's life is singularly perfect, as though just now she has fully absorbed the experience of youth and is taking a deep breath, preparing for wisdom.

The Turner woman was on her porch, wiping her hands furiously on her apron, calling to her children. One of the boys hurried up the steps and mother and son engaged in anxious dialogue. She pointed a finger between his eyes; he gestured towards the yard, the street, the other children, with feckless stammers and sobs. She won the battle through severity and height.

"Let the boy explain," said Annie softly as she watched. "It wasn't his fault. It wasn't his fault at all,"

"Done," said Charlotte, She leaned back, held the drawing tablet before her to evaluate the work; she frowned. "I don't like it. It doesn't capture you, Annie. One day I'll really capture you."

"No doubt," her sister snorted. "I can move now, I assume." Charlotte laughed. "I've only just begun with the sketching. I know I have a lot to learn, but I'm starting to really take risks."

"Well, as long as you're taking risks, dear."

We had just finished supper—I fried chicken and Charlotte baked a syrupy peach pie—and were assembled in Charlotte's room; the sun was setting, the sky of the last of autumn was pale yellow.

I had stretched out on the floor to go through the newspapers of the last few days. Freed from her model-pose, Annie moved dispiritedly to the armchair by the bureau, which was cluttered with small colored glass bottles. Charlotte was on her bed, of course: like one of those impervious old ocean liners floating untroubled in the sea of books, drawing tablets, pencils, her typewriter.

On the bedside table were three juice glasses and a pitcher. "My special evening drink, anyone?" She poured some of the cloudy rust-colored liquid for each of us.

"What is this concoction you drink, Charlotte? A fairy tale potion?"

Charlotte laughed. "Only iced tea, Annie. With a little something to kick it in."

Annie sipped the drink and winced. Charlotte's new passion is fully half as much vodka as tea. Annie's eyes settled absently on Charlotte's bare legs, the pastel pink lines which are the scars, and she looked away.

We passed some moments in silence. Then, Annie said: "Charlotte, I wonder if you've given any thought to what we talked about on the phone?"

"Oh, that. Oh, well, Annie...it's sweet of you. But, I can't. I really can't move down to the city. You know how badly I did when I was there—"

"Yes, but that was ten years ago."

"Too much traffic. Too scary. Things hurt me too much there and I got sad."

Annie's head did not move, but her eyes shifted slowly to see me. I turned a page.

"Really, I know you want to help. But, it's not a very good time.

54

I'm busy. I can't even think of making a transition now; not while I'm working on my book."

The subject of Charlotte's projects always infuriates Annie. She stubbed out her cigarette, took too hearty a swallow of the drink.

"This is to be a book for children," Charlotte went on. "It's all about the different people a little girl meets one day in a walk through her town. They're all angry, sad people."

Annie slid the side of her hand across her forehead and said wearily: "Charlotte, I understand all that."

To me, Charlotte said: "Do you see how somber Annie is? She thinks I'm just crazy."

"No one thinks you're crazy," Annie responded.

"Your husband does, always did."

After a pause and a sip, Annie's face relaxed into a smile.

"Yes. He thinks everyone but him is crazy."

"And I think everyone but me is crazy," said Charlotte cheerily.

We all laughed, but it was short, and the room once again fell silent.

Done with the papers, I wanted to go off to the front room, but felt paralyzed. Annie would have preferred if I left, I think. It isn't really that she resents or dislikes me; perhaps I function as a barrier to things Annie would wish to say to her sister. So, while I thought I should leave them alone together, something kept me there—was I fearful of what would pass between them, trying to monitor or control, or am I just nosy? I lit a cigarette, pulling over one of Charlotte's albums of newspaper clippings to thumb through.

"You know tonight is Spook's Night, don't you?" Charlotte asked.

Annie turned round, smiling. "Is it? I had forgotten all about Spook's Night."

This town tradition dates back to long before any of us were born. Some insipid legend about newlyweds who, while taking a moonlight stroll through the village green, were suddenly enveloped by a harsh wind and a low, sinister hum. The bride shrieked, no doubt, and the groom pulled her close. Before them appeared a presence, transparent, looming, which boldly announced that it was a ghost but would not harm the couple. The ghost declared it would return every year on that exact night. Now, the mission of this ghost, its motivation or message has never been explained and is, finally, unimportant. The sober, peculiar ritual of Spook's Night was begun—Spook's Night involves no costumes or candy, it is not frivolous. People leave their lights on all night. They sit at their windows or on their porches, stand all together in their yards looking vaguely upward, awaiting some flicker of white, a fast motion, the wind and the hum. Naturally, there are those who claim to sense or see something each year; but, generally, when people put their sleepy children to bed and retire themselves just after midnight, it is without disappointment for having missed the ghost; rather, I think we are relieved, reassured to know nothing is really out there.

Charlotte and I have spent many Spook's Nights together; as children, with huge eyes, breathing quickly, and when we got older, we smoked cigarettes and mocked it all.

In fact, there is something truly spooky about Spook's Night: our town becomes deadly silent, thoughtful, as families huddle together, take their places to wait. No child giggles, no parent scolds. The older people peer through their curtains. It is as though for this night we are all praying, acknowledging a mystery of which we are terrified. Charlotte once said: "I believe in ghosts like I believe in God."

Annie rested her head against the back of the chair. "Sidney's found another woman." She touched her cheeks with the palms of her hands, and the gesture was a picture of her marriage: years of accusations and denials, phones being banged onto their cradles, furious pleading, terrible concessions. When they were young, Annie probably cried her eyes out, clutching a pillow; and as the marriage went on, her crying stopped. That's sad.

"Yes," answered Charlotte. "You said so in your letter."

"Another woman. Apparently, women are exchangable. But, he can't have found another me." She laughed and sniffled, let smoke out in a hostile puff.

Charlotte leaned forward and then stretched on her stomach, her elbows propped, her chin in her hands. "Did you ever really trust Sidney?"

"Of course I did. We loved each other. Eleven years. Our marriage was built on trust."

Charlotte was excited, like a schoolgirl who has the arithmetic answer: "But, you *can't* trust anybody. Not in that way, at least. All you can trust people to do is...whatever they're going to do."

I found this remark particularly profound, lovely, so characteristically Charlotte-like. Annie, though, was sarcastic: "Yes, dear, and I know you're so rich with experience in the world of romance, so wise."

"At least I am not exasperated," Charlotte replied, and the sisters laughed. "But, don't you see, really? To me it's so clear that all any one of us has is herself. Vows and agreements and commitments, where do they come from? Where does that word love even come from? That's what I've learned in life: as far as other people go, all you can really count on is that they'll be themselves."

"You do get right to the core of things, Charlotte. You really do."

What is it about Charlotte? Selfishness? A buried, cherished selfishness that literally excludes others from her vision, and exempts her from the pain they may bring with them?

I look for some crushed hopes, great disappointments, humiliations, some ruinous love in Charlotte's story, and do not find them. She never got that far.

Once she told me the reason she does not adore old movies, as I do, is that, with all the tearful farewells and steamy reunions, the serene families, the devotion and passion, the boy getting the girl, movies will make you think there is such a thing as love.

"I'd like to get back to the subject at hand, please," Annie said gruffly, and she stole a fast glance at me. "Is it really such a good idea for you to stay up here, Charlotte? You know, I'd love to have you with me in the city. And the resources there...."

Resources are doctors in Annie's language: psychiatrists to address Charlotte's reclusiveness and medical doctors for the pain in her legs.

Charlotte said: "Do you see that tree outside the window? Those long branches hanging down like a girl's braids? What kind of tree is that?"

"Weeping willow," answered Annie, miserably.

Annie has pressured Charlotte for years about moving back to the city; these days the discussion is more highly charged, I suppose, because Annie herself is lonely and depressed.

Of course, what never gets discussed is me. I am that elephant sitting in the living room which people step gingerly around but will not

57

acknowledge. When they are alone, and Annie is trying to persuade her sister how much better it would be to live in the city, how does Charlotte phrase her answer? That she cannot be without me, or that I cannot be without her?

Annie rose, walked back towards the window. We heard a radio announcer's intonation from the Turner house, and Mrs Turner's frustrated, angry voice rose above it through the stillness.

▼

Night came. It was cool. We had brought three chairs to the open window.

Annie had changed into a nightgown and thick robe and fastened curlers to the end of her hair. Charlotte was wrapped in her favorite afghan. Charlotte worried about me in the draught and insisted I wear gloves and a scarf tight around my neck.

Pictures Charlotte has cut from magazines and tacked to the walls bounced against each other crazily in the quick breeze. The mirrored doors of the wardrobe were partly open, showing the sleeves of all the dresses Charlotte never wears.

The Turners were in their backyard in winter clothes. Mrs Turner cradled an infant, Mr Turner held his little sick daughter against his chest, the other children were joined hand to hand, and the group was illumined by lights from the windows of their home.

"Do you think Mrs Coffee waits for the ghost on Spook's Night?" Charlotte asked.

"Oh, she waits," answered Annie.

"What about that old Mr Hornstein?"

"Everyone waits," said Annie.

"We aren't supposed to talk, you know," I said, but was ignored.

"It's half past eleven," Annie said, lighting another cigarette. "It's almost over."

"Look how the Turners are facing the river," Charlotte said. "Why, I wonder? What makes them think the ghost will come from that direction? Isn't the whole thing so absurd?"

"You know, Charlotte, all I mean is that you can't hide up here in this bedroom forever."

"Should I come to the city just to find a different bedroom to hide in?"

"Maybe you should stop hiding altogether."

"People choose things. You chose your life. Your charities and things, your husband, your daughter—what is her name again?"

"Priscilla," Annie answered, as though admitting a sick secret.

"Yes, Priscilla. I always forget her name. And what kind of carpet, this or that vase, this or that color for the kitchen...."

"What are you saying? What does all this mean?"

Charlotte did not look directly at her sister, nor match Annie's intensity. "That this is my choice. It isn't the best choice, maybe. To stay here, to be here. But, it's a place where I know I will not feel too unhappy."

On the bureau, a candle burned out and fell into its bottle, and smoke curled through the open window, out into the night, away. We three now had our elbows on the window sill.

"Don't be angry with me, Annie," Charlotte said.

"I'm not angry, I'm not. Around you I feel so damned defensive all the time. I'm concerned about you."

"No, you shouldn't be."

"You know, I have a *good* life going for me, Charlotte."

I can remember Annie heading down the hill to the train station the day she left for college. Charlotte and I carried her new maroon luggage. About to board, one foot on the step, Annie raised an arm—her dress had flowers and frilly sleeves—and we expected her to say, I will miss you Charlotte, Goodbye Charlotte, I love you Charlotte. What she said was: "Be good, you two."

Charlotte's response was a fast, withering stare of contradictions, at once scolding and forgiving; somehow Charlotte was suddenly older. Her look did not plead: Do not abandon me, do not abandon me. It was a declaration: Oh, *you* cannot abandon *me*.

I wonder about Annie's own recollection of that moment when she left her sister behind; at college, with some special girlfriend, exchanging deep confidences and serious, cozy gossip, analyzing life, planning, filling ashtrays, and in the morning hoarse and gratified, was she always remembering that extraordinary expression on Charlotte's face?

The sisters are such a contrast. Charlotte has struggled to comprehend;

she has investigated, she has questioned. Annie, it seems, has always known. Charlotte responds to pain, while Annie glides past and through, achieving, asserting. Annie's beautiful, cold stare shows so little doubt about what is right and wrong and true. But, Charlotte's perspicacious uncertainty has cast a spell on Annie, as it has on me. Annie must fear, as I do, being stripped skinless.

▼

It was almost midnight. When the talk is in whispers and it's dark, you can forget you are a grownup.

"What is death, Annie?"

"No one knows."

"But, what do you think?"

"No, Charlotte. No, what do *you* think?"

"All right, then. That death is the absolute end. There is nothing after this life. There's no soul. And people endlessly hope that they will continue on after their bodies are cracked bones rotting in a box underground. But, that's just a story. This is the life. When this ends, there is no more."

Annie was stiff at her shoulders, her eyes were tired. "That's a scary thing for people, Charlotte. You can see why people hope there's something more."

Charlotte was alert, she sat erect. "I know, I *know*. That's what's so fascinating about the whole thing. What people will do or not do. Because I think deep down inside, everyone knows. Everyone in their lonely, true heart knows—don't you think?—that this existence is the ultimate one. So people race around madly, looking for happiness, and it's such a terrible, huge challenge, and we're not ready for it...."

Annie seemed suddenly distracted, irritated. Thinking about what train to catch in the morning, perhaps, or her daughter or a phone call she meant to make, or the last nasty thing her ex-husband had said. "It's midnight now. No ghost. I have to get to bed."

Annie held her robe at the neck and stepped lightly towards the door. She said good night in a whisper, arching her brow.

I said good night, too, and went to the couch where I've been sleeping during Annie's visit. Charlotte remained at her window, leaning out. I suppose she watched the Turner family leave its post. And stayed there a while longer, as lights were turned out, doors were locked; Charlotte, an untroubled witness to our whole town in its brave, sad concealment.

Winter

Seven

Last night, I dreamed about moors layered with a forest of wild, tough heather, and I am lost, but not anxious. Charlotte appears. She tells me she's bored. I say: "But, you're never bored." We laugh. Charlotte says: "So, *these* are the moors." I woke thirsty.

There has always been so much about Cathy and Heathcliff with which we identify. We first picked up the book as youngsters. Its emotion was raw, could not be concealed, and spooky and complex; above all, it was enduring emotion.

I can picture us now, sitting on a couple of rocks at the river's edge, and can hear Charlotte's pretend English accent and her passion as she read aloud to me: " 'I cannot express it; but surely you and everybody have a notion that there is or should be an existence of yours beyond you. What were the use of my creation, if I were entirely contained here? My great miseries in this world have been Heathcliffs miseries, and I watched and felt each from the beginning: my great thought in living is himself. If all else perished, and *he* remained, I should still continue to be; and if all else remained, and he were annihilated, the universe would turn to a mighty stranger: I should not seem a part of it.' " And when she got to her favorite line—when Catherine cries: "Nelly, I *am* Heathcliff!"— Charlotte gripped the weathered volume, a breeze swept her hair, she was so magnificent.

As adolescents we felt we belonged fully to that world of Bronte's story: where you are buried in sight of your family home, whole lives are spent with the same relations and servants and sky, where peace is found in death and the world you imagine is the world in which you live.

▼

Winter is here. The first snow fell at midnight and melted during the day. The roads are lines of tire tracks now, dirty white. Some of the Turner children, bound in scarves and coats and galoshes, were let loose in their yard to throw handfuls of wet ice at each other and finally one was hit in the neck, cried, called for its tormented mother.

I walked to the movie in town this afternoon—Hitchcock's *Rear Window,* a film I never tire of. On my way home, I stopped at the post office. Peg Pelliteer was gross and petulant, reprimanding that poor old man who drives the mail truck (I think he is a little slow). She plopped down a bundle of mail for us and I did not look at it until I reached home.

Charlotte was glazing a ham with Coca-Cola. "I've heard it brings out the natural juices or something," she told me.

I looked through the letters, filed all the bills, to be turned over to Aunt Kaye later. I came upon an envelope addressed to me, from Mr Cole at XXX Press, Inc. I gazed at it, tore its edge slowly, pulled out the handwritten note. I read it twice.

Charlotte was on her knees before the open oven attaching pineapple slices to the ham with toothpicks. "Charlotte, there's a note here. Charlotte, listen, guess what?" She looked over her shoulder at me. She was smiling. "They want my book," I said. "They do want it. I mean, they say they *might,* anyway. This Mr Cole says he was intrigued—wait a second—'I found myself especially intrigued with the Gothic, dreamy quality of your novel,' he says. And he says he has a couple of suggestions, he'd like to discuss it." I frantically scanned the lines of the letter. "Mr Cole wants to meet with me soon, go over some changes and sign a contract."

"A contract!"

I stood in the center of the kitchen, the page from Cole trembling between my fingers, and Charlotte did not move, nor change her pleased expression. I swung in a little circle, thrilled, and went back into the front room to pull out my manuscript and hold it tight.

The ham just tasted sugary and dried out. Charlotte was silent and strange during supper, almost shy. I wonder if she is envious. Or perhaps my smug expression was simply annoying to her. I do feel so satisfied.

▼

This winter, this weak snowfall, marks a decade since I had that trouble at school. I was a fairly pretty boy, thin and unhappy. I sipped sherry, alone in my dormitory room. I composed experimental poems. I missed Charlotte, who was living in the city then. We wrote and talked by phone.

The college was a sprawling complex of cement buildings and parking spaces, plopped down in the middle of a prosperous valley. Structures were continually being added: a gymnasium, an auditorium, new dormitories, and I recall the giant cranes swinging over the quadrangle, signifying our rich future.

Students were angry and naive, occasionally tragic. Once in a while there would be a suicide or a drug overdose, and all of us would stare at the pavement as we walked to classes, keep silent in the dining hall, avoiding each other's eyes so we would not have to see our shared confusion, and know that these scholars were terrified children still.

The bulldozers had not killed selected patches of wood and grass. There was a path through a thicket behind the brand new Natural Sciences building which was notorious as a pick-up spot for men. During my first semester I heard about the night-time activity in those bushes, but I stayed away.

That semester, I wrote papers on Gide and Mann. By my second semester though, I was devouring Jean Genet and felt ready to walk into the woods.

I had a good pal at school, Douglas: he studied Marx, was rather humorless. We decided to pursue the sexual darkness together late one night. Thorns pricked through our jeans as we affected a casual stroll along the uneven pathway. I was fearful, breathing rapidly, my eyes were wide, straining to see; but, as there was no one near, no sound, my anxiety abruptly became disappointment.

Douglas and I stood still, and for one absurd moment a current passed between us, touched by sex, smelling of something erotic, but it dissolved. Much more comfortable as partners in this adventure. We looked away from each other.

Leaves rustled, our heads jerked. I lit a cigarette. My knees were weak and shivering, and I tried to hide it. I saw a form to the left, Douglas saw one ahead. A figure shot past us. There were indeed men out here, we realised, shadowmen.

Douglas and I returned to our dorm rooms calmly, slowly, but in our hearts we were running and gleeful. The next night, a Friday, after a gulp of my beloved, glamorous sherry, I went back to the bushes, alone. I could see students walking on the sidewalk, on their way to the new auditorium for a film screening. I stood still, my shadow cast long in front of me by the moon.

A man nudged past me on the path, coughed and said: "Excuse me," and headed further back. I wanted to follow, I wanted to go deeper, but was frozen.

The man was suddenly near me again. He circled me, lit a cigarette. I was awkward, trying for some insouciant, sexy pose. The man disappeared and returned again, stood facing me, but I could not see his eyes. I heard some girls laughing far away.

In one breezy motion, the man tossed his cigarette onto the path and put his hands on my shoulders. He guided me back a few steps, then pressed against me. I still could not see him, so I closed my eyes and felt him. He was strong, thick, knowing. He kissed my neck, then my lips, then nudged his hand behind my belt and into my trousers.

When I was back in my room that night and had taken more sherry, I wrote a few macabre lines of poetry. I was thrilled with my experience; it was like a shot of darkness and risk, right into a vein. It had added to my spirit.

I spoke often to Charlotte from the pay telephone in the dorm hallway, and I'd scratch marks with a pencil on the wall. She was fascinated with the idea of anonymous sexual assignations. "Do you just sort of prowl around looking at each other?" she asked.

I answered: "Sometimes we can barely see each other, really."

"And what is it you are searching for?"

"It's sex, Charlotte. Purely sex."

"But, they're lonely, aren't they? And aren't some of them married men who are hiding that they're homosexual?"

"Some are, I guess." I felt and showed a sophisticated distance from Charlotte. "People do things for all kinds of reasons. These places exist everywhere, you know. There's a whole backroom-bushes society— specific men's rooms, certain rest-stops along certain highways. It's a very evolved underground world. And the thing is," I explained, impatient, "it's only for sex."

"Intimacy is no part of this kind of thing, then?"

And I said: "Right. This is the kind of thing where you don't have to care. This has nothing to do with intimacy," but now perhaps I think differently. I have had many of these adventures, quick, cunning sex scenes in dark public places. I have been promiscuous, I suppose, if numerous encounters with strangers makes one promiscuous; although if I had had many sexual encounters with one person I'd just be called faithful. But something does happen in the bushes and backrooms, some closeness. It can't be love, because love seems to take time; but, it is virtually love.

The following Monday I started my new creative writing course. I had heard nothing but the importance of getting in Professor Everson's class, and how brilliant he was, what an exciting instructor. The enrollment was limited, and I actually prayed that I would be one of the fortunate few, and I was.

Everson arrived late, sat cross-legged on the table in the front of the room. He was young, his hair was uncombed. He had round, wire-rimmed glasses and a strong chin. Describing methods of character development, he spoke slowly, peevishly, as though to imbeciles. A young woman asked a question and Everson blinked hard, winced, shook his head, confounded. The unnerved young woman slouched in her seat and chewed on a bit of her hair.

Everson ended our first class by warning us all about his exacting standards, and that he was never going to favor kindness over truth. "In my course," he told us, "those of you who think you are writers will find out how wrong you are."

Everson's arrogance sparked my own, and terror. I was deciding not to return to his class. It was not until this disenchanted, humiliated group was filing out, past his desk to pick up copies of the syllabus, that I recognized Everson's posture, noticed a familiar smell or movement: he was my man from the bushes.

Charlotte loved this development. "Are you sure? Positive? And do you think he knows who you are? Does he know you know?"

A week or two passed, and I have forgotten the details of how Everson and I acknowledged each other. One day I kidded him about his tie, I think. And another day he asked to join me at lunch in the dining hall.

Our conversation was stiff. He frowned and was grumpy. If I mentioned a writer who interested me, Everson rolled his eyes.

Finally, one night he took me for a drive and we ended up at a gay bar some sixty miles south of school, the only one in the area. Standing with our vodka and grapefruits under rotating red lights, he talked about the book he was writing, a study of Dostoevsky's work. As the evening went on and we got looser from the drinks he told me he was only teaching so he could flirt with the boys, and we laughed.

Everson and I spent quite a few nights together at his apartment in town, two narrow rooms with a low ceiling, cluttered with books and barbells. He was voluble, smoked and drank wine. He was extraordinarily concerned and impatient about his career—getting published, getting tenure, disagreements with others on the faculty, slights he'd felt from the administration. I told Charlotte: "He's so young to be so bitter."

I was flattered to be with him, and so could not even notice that I did not like him much. He was calculating with sex, lots of cooing and moaning; he stretched full on the bed, waiting to be worshipped; he handled my penis roughly, like he was angry about something. And when we'd part, Everson would ask: "When will we see each other again?" but I heard no affection in his tone, it was more an accusation.

He sweet-talked me into things. We were a little drunk, naked on his bed; the room was dark but for an illuminated green dial on his stereo; he whispered: "I want to fuck you."

"I don't know," I said.

"It's okay, okay," he said, pushing his hands through my hair, kissing my neck. But a few moments later: "Oh, I really would love to fuck you. You're so soft, so pretty."

Charlotte's opinion of Everson, based upon this exchange, was that he was a typical dangerous man: manipulative yet enticing, handsome but uncaring. She said: "It will be very sad if you fall under his spell."

Our affair had been going on for a month or so. It was a few days before school was to close for the Christmas break. I got a phone call from Everson. He said he could not keep our date that night and would be busy the next few days. He would see me after the holidays.

My brilliant and beautiful short story concerned a boy and his mother: the mother is an artist, a sculptor (I referred to her as a sculptress) and they live on the beach and the mother is a sort of free spirit who takes in a handsome sailor and the son is wracked with jealousy and confusion and finally breaks all his mother's clay heads. I can't even remember from where I stole this droll tale; but, stylistically, I think I was being Gertrude Stein, repeating a lot.

When Everson returned the six or seven pages to me, the margins were stained with his mean red pen. "Laughable." "Ridiculous." "Where is the boy's father?" "Does this boy not go to school?" "This business with the clay heads is the most trite and least effective kind of symbolism." Question marks and explanation points, scratched right across the text. His final assessment was that some of the dialogue was amusing, and the grade was a D.

Charlotte was home from the city for Christmas, and I had come down from school. Her present to me was a beautiful porcelain sleeping cat. I had not held it for even a minute when it dropped and shattered. I burst out crying.

"Crying over this dumb cat?" Charlotte asked, trying to meet my eyes, but my head was lowered. "Here," she said, "forget about this dumb cat." She collected the chips and fragments and put them in one of her father's empty tobacco tins and handed it to me. "Merry Christmas," she said and we laughed.

When I returned to school, various versions of the news had already spread: Professor Everson had resigned, had been asked to resign, had actually been fired.

I got a note summoning me to the plant-filled office of the Dean of Humanities and Arts, Mrs Spottiswode, a tweedy, gentle woman, quite out of place as an administrator. She read to me from the records of Everson's hearing with the board. A student from the previous year had claimed he'd been pressured into sexual relations with the professor. Mrs Spottiswode hardly looked at me as she went over the many sound reasons that faculty and students are forbidden to become entangled. "It is a very serious charge," she said.

I was alarmed, and could not discover what she knew of my affair with Everson. "Am I being kicked out of school or something, Mrs Spottiswode?"

"Well, no. Certainly not." She seemed exhausted, then.

After a silence, I asked: "And why are you telling all of this to me?"

She shrugged. "I don't really know. We thought you would be interested. You're taking cinema courses this semester, I see."

As I walked across that silly campus, I knew it was already a bad memory: my pain came less from feelings about Everson, more from the sudden and total failure of my short story. I was, I concluded, one of those who thought he was a writer and had learned how wrong he was.

If I felt only defeated, Charlotte, just home from her miserable time in the city, felt gifted with clarity. "We must not accept anything—*anything*—in place of love," she declared. Charlotte had learned some truth, I could see it in her eyes. She'd made a decision: to find a home.

I finished my semester with enthusiasm for nothing except the Happy Hour at the cocktail lounge in town. By sunset every day I was passed out drunk in my room, and by midnight I was wide awake, everything sore—my joints, my eyes, even my hair. And though my thoughts were foggy, one thing was distinct, a beaming certain truth: I will fail.

I received a letter some months later from Everson, who'd moved to Boston. He said he had been going through difficulties for quite a while, that his judgment was affected, that he was taking time to think, and he hoped I had not been hurt. He said nothing about my story. His closing remark was a strange, sad mixture of teacherly superiority and real sincerity: "You are a nice, bright young man. I pray you will remember me."

I have held onto that note, kept it in the tobacco tin with the broken bits of the sleeping cat.

Eight

The relentless chill and bright white of winter is a hardship. I have to wear a scarf, gloves and a cap over my ears or my teeth chatter.

A few days ago, Jesse and I met for coffee at the cafe in the city. He asked, bluntly, if I'd taken the test. "Well, yes, actually. Last year. My test...my test came back positive."

I searched that sweet face for a sign of hesitation or doubt. He said nothing for several seconds and then: "Are you scared?"

Affecting infinite sobriety and calm, I explained that I have known my health status for some time and feel adjusted to it. I said that I regularly see a doctor and have, in fact, been completely free of symptoms and illness. I get blood tests once a month, I explained. My eyes insisted I was coping and that my head was clear. Jesse put his hand on mine and smiled. I shrugged my shoulders; I don't know why.

I had not, of course, really answered his question. I did not tell Jesse that every sniffle or ache forms sadness and worry, that every bland newspaper account of this spreading plague is a blow to my spirit.

Those photographs of skinny men hooked up to machines—that will be me. The grim statistics sweep me away from all I know and the good things I've been waiting for. The epidemic is not merely this decade's news; it is my future. My generation is rapidly losing weight. Africa is disappearing, and I'll go along with it. I could not tell Jesse that those rejection notes, with their terse couple of lines, which every writer learns to crumple and toss away, represent to me a race, a challenge, evidence of how I am being cheated and deprived. My plans are squashed. I have always known, for example, that at the age of fifty, I'd write the masterpiece, the long, brave novel, and critics and biographers would then assess the work of my twenties, thirties and forties. This and all other scenarios of a full, rich life have fallen away now.

Will I be alive long enough to be mature? I mean, long enough to possess that generous kind of smile that accepts the world a bit more?

At night, when Charlotte is drinking her cocoa and reading, I cannot sleep; voices chatter questions in each ear. At this time next year, how will I look and sound? Will I be able to move, to see, to think? Will a day come when I am not even able to read? And about sex—freedom and pleasure that I have not yet really been able to know, maybe I will not know. My expression must be just like that of a hungry child staring at plates of food.

In some sinister way, Jesse is a plate of food. I could not love him; I envy too much what he has. I do not feel safe beside him. So I never said that I am waiting for my last breath, waiting, and, yes, of course, I *am* scared.

▼

Last night, Charlotte and I had the sort of exchange which I adore so much, which summons all of my affection for her, and for myself—for us both. We were at the kitchen table, and I felt a bit testy toward her. Charlotte was describing a television documentary she'd seen about how police dust for fingerprints, but she had some of the facts wrong.

Then, my eyes got glassy and unfocused and I said: "I'm having *deja vu*."

"No, really?" Charlotte asked. She slapped her crossed legs with the palms of her hands. "I am too, we're having it at the same time."

We laughed, and it did feel we had said these words and had this laugh before.

"I still feel it," Charlotte whispered.

"*I* still feel it."

We relived our spooky, mutual moment, staring at each other.

"Oh," said I, "it's gone now."

"Yes. It's gone."

▼

Hornstein's store, a weathered two-room house, sits at the edge of dense, black woods. On its roof, a sign reads:

74

HORNSTEIN'S GENERAL MERCHANDISE
Bait & Tackle—Liquor—Notary Public

Beside the stone porch a rusted automobile is raised on cinder blocks. Two wooden planks form a bridge from the road to the house, across a yard which in summer is merely a bog of mud and in winter is frozen, black earth.

Mr Hornstein orders special cream for Charlotte. One early morning a week or so ago, I stopped by to pick it up. The store was empty. The screen door slapped loud behind me, but no one appeared.

I heard a cough from the back room, which is separated from the store by a brown curtain. "Mr Hornstein? Are you open yet, Mr Hornstein?" I called.

He pushed his head around the curtain then, saw me and stepped out. "Yes, oh yes," he said. He was holding a wooden box under one arm. "I'm open. I've been going through my cash and accounts. But I've got the cream for Miss Charlotte. And does she need any bandages or tape?"

I shook my head. He turned from me and opened an enormous drawer filled with paper bags, pulled out one with Charlotte's name on it.

I handed Mr Hornstein a five dollar bill. "Now let's see," he said, unlatching the wooden box and sliding its top off. Inside were bundles of bills, several notebooks, receipts, pencils, rubber bands. "Let's see, yes, here's some ones." He stripped two dollar bills from their stack and handed them across to me. "And, let's see, seventeen cents also I owe you."

The coins were kept in peppermint tins inside the giant wooden box, and as Mr Hornstein was shifting the tins about, looking for my change, I saw a dark stripe on his forearm, covered by thick grey hair. He counted out a dime, a nickel, two pennies, slapped the coins on the counter.

"There you go, young man, to the last cent." Mr Hornstein grinned. He leaned his elbow against the glass counter-top. I looked quickly at his arm once again, and I know he saw the direction of my glance, but he said nothing, did not move. I thanked him and left the store.

I was back at Hornstein's this morning and tripped on a loose board before the doorway. "Oh, careful, careful," Mr Hornstein said, rushing towards me. I told him I was just fine.

Mr Hornstein called: "David, come out here right at once." Mr

75

Hornstein's son stepped through the curtain from the back room. "David, you'll get the truck going, we'll take this young man down to the clinic and have them give an X-ray."

David only looked at me, sleepy and confused.

"I really am fine. Just lost my balance. There's nothing to worry about, Mr Hornstein."

"I know, I know, but sometimes these things are very serious."

"I'm sure I'm all right."

David was wearing faded denim bib-overalls; his chest and feet were bare and dark; his hair was deep black, curled. He stood with his hands together before an electric heater.

David is a year older than I. He was a hero in high school, the kind I paid little attention to, an athlete and a beauty, the tallest, the strongest, wreathed in everyone's praise and envy. I remember the principal, a skinny red-haired man, as year after year he handed ribbons and medals to this prize boy, this perfect boy—and his gaze, which others took as fondness or awe or pride, Charlotte and I were certain was lust. David went off to college, but soon returned home to help his father at the store.

David stepped towards me, looked me over, held my shoulder with one hand. "Sure nothing got broken?" he asked with rigid seriousness.

"Yes, it's silly. I am just fine."

David glared at me for another second, and then must have been satisfied for he turned and walked back across the store and through the curtain. My eyes followed his figure—broad shoulders, slender legs—and then noticed tiny, old Mr Hornstein standing before me.

Mr Hornstein stepped around and behind his counter: it was his spot, the position of his trade, one of complete confidence and strength.

He rested his left arm on the glass jar which holds licorice. Hornstein's has sold black and red string licorice since before I was born. There was that mark on his arm again: a greenish-black rectangle.

"Oh, yes," Mr Hornstein said. "Some people, the worst they ever get is a scratch from their little kitty cat, and it leaves a scar. But, I have this forever and ever." He was smiling, blinking fast.

I looked from his wet, heavy eyes to his arm, and the mark seemed sharper, brighter.

"Numbers. You see?" He extended his arm across the counter.

"Tattooed onto my skin. They don't wash off, oh no." Mr Hornstein spoke as though to a child, and perhaps he still thinks of me as a child. "From the war," he went on. "They came to our town, pulled us all together and put the women and the children on a train. Many miles."

In the back room, David turned on the radio.

"And they kept the men all together in a separate train and we were taken to another place, away from our families." He put his index finger to his lips and tapped twice. "Those trains were very crowded and cold. I'll never forget."

Now he absently drew a small circle on the glass with the palm of his hand. "I had a sister, a young girl. I was sure she would survive, because she was so angry." Mr Hornstein coughed a laugh. "She was bitter and just so angry, she shook her fist at the soldiers, pulled at their buttons. But, I learned later she had died." He turned from me, began unloading a box of crackers onto a shelf as he spoke. "People who were not there, you know, how can they ever really know what it was like? They just hear the stories, they feel bad. So, that's fine. It's the way it changes you, though. To be young, to see your life, everything you know, your family, the whole world destroyed and there's nothing to do. What can you do?" He was reaching to a high shelf but now looked over his shoulder. "You accept the world is the way it is, and then you get mad and try and make it better." He snorted a laugh, then sighed and put his hands on his lower back.

I asked: "How old were you then, Mr Hornstein?"

"Twenty. Just twenty when they came to our town."

I had nothing to say. The curtain was pushed aside and David edged his shoulder and face through. "I'm going into town for those nails. Anything else you need?" David was frowning.

"You know what we could use? Some little cherry candies." To me, he said: "I like to have the little cherry candies for the youngsters, you know." Mr Hornstein has always been especially nice to the children of the town.

David put on his coat. He offered to drive me home but I said I'd walk. He held a battered paperback book in his coat pocket which, as he turned, I saw was *Gone With The Wind*.

Mr Hornstein had Charlotte's supplies ready, as he always does.

"You'll tell Miss Charlotte hello from me."

I was careful making my way back across the little bridge. I saw the Hornstein truck bouncing over rocks on the narrow road, headed towards town.

How I had hurried to escape Mr Hornstein's testimony, his violent remembrances interrupted by chuckles and coughing. He has always seemed just this old: I do not remember darker hair or a stronger, more youthful posture, or a time when the planes of his cheeks were not creased. I do not remember those numbers on his arm.

I wonder if Charlotte knows about Mr Hornstein, that he was captured, taken from his home, brutalized, that he lives with and must always bear the memories and impact of a war. It is the kind of fact she would know, and which hurts her so deeply; more evidence in support of her own conclusions, that life is a thing one suffers through and endures.

And she will be amused to hear that that striking, mysterious, dreamy David Hornstein is reading *Gone With The Wind*.

▼

Our arrangement was to meet in the city, on the steps of the museum at noon, and I was there, but Jesse was late. Jesse has been late to all of our meetings. At half past, I saw his bicycle swerving carelessly through pedestrians on the sidewalk, and he stopped in front of me.

He lives a block from the museum; the building was once a warehouse and has now been converted into lofts. Jesse and his bicycle and I rode one of those old elevators with a gate and crashed to a squeaky halt at the fifth floor.

He preceded me inside. I stood uncertainly, my hands tucked into my jacket pockets. One wall was made entirely of smoky glass windows running from floor to ceiling; it muted the daylight, throwing bronze shadows on the dusty, damaged wooden floor. A mattress was on the floor in a corner, sheets draped across it. In the opposite corner were a large basin and a counter with a toaster, a hot plate, a stack of dishes. There were some empty picture frames and a mirror leaning against a wall. There were two or three cardboard boxes in the center of the room, a pile of clothes, newspapers, and then I saw an orange cat, mean-looking and too thin. And dust everywhere; this was the kind of place which would always have dust, could never be completely clean.

"Well?" Jesse demanded, grinning, holding out his arms.

I said it certainly was very big.

"Yes, and, well, it isn't done yet or anything. I'm going to fix it up." He stood before each wall then, describing where shelves and cupboards and closets will go, using his hands to measure space, and said that he plans eventually to put his bed on stilts.

We sat on the mattress and shared a bottle of soda. I looked for books, and there were none. Jesse pulled off his shirt and took one of my cigarettes. He reached in a box at the end of the bed and withdrew two small blue pills, popped them in his mouth, swallowed fast.

I asked: "How old are you?"

"Twenty."

This information froze me. I think I have a fear of anyone younger than I; but, obviously, also an attraction. It is that someone twenty years old is of a world completely separate from mine. We can never meet, I think. We are not aligned. Living for so long with Charlotte has spoiled me; perhaps I am so used to her, I can't help but search for her. Mutual deja vu is, after all, such a rare thing.

"So, I think I'll paint the floor bright, bright red," Jesse was saying.

With these resentments of my own limitations in mind, I struck out with an enthusiastic response. "Great idea, great." But, it was lame.

Through our three or four meetings, I have heard Jesse's aspirations and plans: he wants to write a play (the convoluted plot of which I could hardly understand), he wants to sing professionally (Gershwin and Brecht), he loves children and thinks he might adopt one someday (with a lesbian pal), he has never been to Brazil but *feels* it is the place for him to live, he is presently "studying" Zen Buddhism and other spiritual stuff.

When I finally did tell Charlotte about Jesse, all she said was: "What a character."

And then he placed his hand on my neck, squeezed, pulled me closer. I noticed his eyes were just the littlest bit crossed. His smile was arrogant and generous and youthful; his arm encircled me, his hair fell across his forehead; it was a carefree, heedless motion, and I felt so lost.

We were stretched out, peeling clothes. Car horns honked outside.

Jesse turned me over, fast and with a grunt, and I saw that horrid cat glaring at me. A puff of dust settled on us. Jesse's kiss was wet and his teeth clicked against mine. He undid my fly and reached inside, but was having trouble maneuvering; my arm was caught underneath me and I couldn't catch my breath.

I had to laugh. I pushed his shoulders, moved him away and sat upright.

"What?" Jesse challenged.

"No, I...it's nothing...I was getting..."

He fit a cigarette and scowled. He took another pill, a yellow one this time.

We sat in silence for quite a while. I wanted to whisper in one of those oversize ears: Jesse, I wish I was you.

My romance is a comedy. And I thought, I really am not all that much older than Jesse; so how can he be so much younger than I? This is the kind of puzzle I know Charlotte will fully appreciate.

I never have thought the day would come when I would not seek an escapade. Is this what being thirty years old means? I do not feel mature at all. Only a sense of mourning for a former adventurousness which, anyway, I never truly had. What do I want in my life? I have huge expectations and desires about this book of mine; sometimes I think about teaching at the college (and flirting with the male students); I no longer crave falling in love, as I once did, but I would like coziness and to be content and amused with someone; and none of these things is really as pressing as my wish to re-pot and rearrange the geraniums on our back porch; I haven't attended to them properly. It's so sad to lose my grandiosity. It's as though my spirit has been mortgaged.

Jesse is bound to ask me. What is your novel about? I'll muse. My novel, I'll tell him, is about identity.

Nine

This morning was crackling, cold, but bright. As I was taking my walk the fire station sent out its hysterical whistle alarm. The truck was made ready, two or three of the town men raced down the hill while struggling to get their rubber jackets on. The truck wheeled out but was back in a moment. Another false alarm.

Peg Pelliteer and the Turner woman—best friends now, it seems—had come out to the post office stoop in response to all the commotion. As we three stood watching the truck and its defeated, discouraged heroes return, Peg Pelliteer lit a cigarette, picked a bit of tobacco from a tooth with her ring finger and thumb, and said: "I don't know if either of you remembers Charlie Farley. Well, he was the little fellow who worked at the railroad station. Now, this was many years ago and that station was a busy place, because back then people were coming and going by train more, and now they all have cars.

"Well, all right, this fellow name of Charlie Farley—never will I forget that silly name he had—was real mild-mannered, real quiet. He had these orange teeth, but he didn't smile much. He'd be all dressed up, neat as a pin in his little railroad suit, that dark blue with the red tie that they had to wear and his little name tag: Charlie Farley. And his little cap. I always thought he was bald maybe under that cap. And he was the one you got your ticket from and who told you when the train was due and like that, so one time or another, pretty much everyone had come across this Charlie Farley. And he was the kind of person you just didn't like. From first sight. He lived here in town with his mother, and people liked *her* well enough, I guess. But he was just this real orderly kind of person, always making little notations. And when he'd say the announcements about the trains coming in on such and such a track, his voice was just nasal and high-pitched. Well, I mean, just everybody hated this man. And nobody really knew him. You couldn't say what you exactly didn't like about him, or why. You just hated him. Because you just did.

"So, one morning I picked up my newspaper like I always did—I don't read the papers anymore—and what's on the front page but a photo of this little mouse face of Charlie Farley. And what was it all about? Well, this little guy had sat down to supper one night with his mother and handed the mother a chunk of steak and some corn and potatoes or whatever and she had dropped dead right on the spot. And they came to find out Charlie Farley had put enough horse tranquilizer in that food to kill an elephant twice the size of his mother.

"And the strange thing is, he'd poisoned his own supper, too, but then changed his mind, didn't take a bite, just watched his own mother gulping down this poison beef. Can you imagine such a thing?

"I remember, I said at the time, that I had always hated that little mouse Charlie Farley. And never knew why I did hate him, but always hated him. Now, I don't even read the papers." Peg Pelliteer flipped her cigarette butt, smoked to the bitter end, onto the curb, shrugged and walked back inside her post office. Mrs Turner stole a glance at me; neither of us knew what to say.

As I headed up the hill towards home I was overwhelmed with distaste for this petty little town, and a sublime vision of myself walking fast along a city street, on my way to an important business appointment or meeting friends for coffeejuggling lovers and trying to make time for all the people and commitments of my varied, intense life.

By the time I reached our front steps I had bitterly sketched a picture of myself as trapped in this wretched place, locked in a haunted house with crazy Charlotte. I was furious at being deprived of all the city offers: handsome sneering boys, women with lots of lipstick, snazzy hotels, trolleys, pollution and prostitutes and flower shops and danger, the constant talk and traffic, a noise like God humming....

And there was Charlotte, serenely alphabetizing the books. I went to my room and shut the door hard.

At supper, Charlotte was sitting on the drainboard of the sink, smoking. I told her of Peg Pelliteer's bizarre narrative, all about Charlie Farley, and we laughed particularly at the phrase, "enough horse tranquilizer to kill an elephant twice the size of his mother."

"You see?" Charlotte said when I was done. "It's *such* a strange thing about people. That they are compelled to tell such awful stories."

▼

Busy couple of days. On Monday, I went for a series of blood tests at the city hospital. Fortunately, the nurse I like was on duty, Brenda. She's overweight and has red hair. "Roll up your sleeve now, honey," she says. I think nurses *should* call the patients 'honey.' Even so, these tests are always a morbid ordeal. The results will not be in for three or four days. And when they are in, what then? If my liver function is up or down or whatever, what do I do? Positives, negatives, ratios—this swirling activity in my blood over which I and science are completely powerless.

Then, Tuesday was my meeting with Mr Cole from XXX Press, Inc. The office was one room divided by a partition. On one side sat a busty, stern-faced woman with plain brown hair parted on the side, plastered to her head like a bathing cap. On her desk was a name plate which read: Ms Vera Wharton. She fiddled with file folders and made check marks on a pad of paper, and somehow I reckoned she really was manufacturing this occupation, that actually she had nothing to do but wait for the phone to ring. Finally, an obnoxious honk came from the antiquated intercom machine. She made a show of pressing the buzzer, and then of ushering me around the partition to be seen by Mr Cole. (Charlotte, greatly anguished, believes that everyone is so sad; I, mildly amused, believe that everyone is just ridiculous.)

Mr Cole was sitting at an ominously clutter-free grey metal desk, under a framed print of a ship on a rolling green sea. He wears very thick glasses, has uncombed and oily greying hair and a beard, chubby cheeks with branches of thin red blood vessels. He hides his big ball of a stomach under a knitted sweater.

"Now then," he said, gruff and kind; he's like some Dickens character. "There are just a couple of problems here with your manuscript, well, we don't even have to call them problems, we can call them situations, or, let's say, questions. The dialogue is extraordinary, very strong. And the mood—the way you've created the mood and captured it and explored it, I really couldn't even put a name to it, but it's very powerful."

Mr Cole coughed. I waited.

83

"What's problematical, or, let's call it questionable, to me, is the pacing. Do you understand? Not much really happens, does it? By that I mean, the standard logic of novels being that somehow, in some way, the characters, or one of the characters, undergoes some sort of change, sees some light, learns some lesson. Which is not to say I don't understand or appreciate the more *avant garde* types of writing. Matter of fact—" here he looked across to some books on a shelf and beamed with pride—"I had my own little romance with the structuralists." He told me that XXX Press, Inc. was the first to publish translations of some obscure French poet. "A shocking, brilliant series of sketches. The first was *Vaginas*. Then came *Scrotums*. Then *Testicles*. Etcetera."

His intercom buzzed. Vera's strident, cheerless, high-pitched voice could be heard perfectly clearly above the partition, but Mr Cole clicked the buttons on the intercom for speaking and listening. "Yes, Vera?"

"Did you want anything else when I go out for the photocopies?"

"No, thank you, Vera. That will be all."

"Fine, Mr Cole. I'll be leaving shortly."

"Very good then."

"All right."

They signed off.

I struggled to brighten my eyes; every facet of this meeting had clouded them with discouragement and doubt. "So, basically, it's the plot that concerns you."

He pounded the ends of his fingers on the desk. "That's it. That's basically it. The plot does not move...do you see what I'm getting at? You seem to let your characters wander, wander in and around. You give them these monologues. And then, of course, the ending does not satisfy. One is left hanging, waiting. Your characters are colorful, they're offbeat, they hold one's interest. And one finds oneself thinking: all right, what will happen to these marvelous characters, now? Oh, excuse me just a moment." He pressed an intercom button. "Vera? Vera?"

Vera, having probably already put on her coat, did not even bother with any mechanical pretense, but bellowed: "Yes, Mr Cole?"

"Vera, it's very urgent that the letter to Ms Glass get out in the morning mail."

"Yes, I have it right here," Vera muttered resentfully.

He turned to me again. "Ms Glass is an exceptionally fine poet, a rare poet. We are very anxious to issue a small volume of her work, but she is very reclusive, she never leaves her house at all, she's a little mad, and then she'll just send bits or pieces and she won't respond to our communications. Very frustrating. She writes and writes, but she does not seem to care at all if anyone reads her work."

An enviable attitude, I thought.

Mr Cole handed his copy of my manuscript across the desk. I turned up the title page and saw red pen markings on page 1. Casually, covertly, I turned to other pages, and there were notes in margins, lines through sentences, question marks and arrows.

Mr Cole chuckled. "Now, that may look awfully messy to you at first. Those are just some of my little suggestions, just the ideas here and there which popped into my mind. Maybe some things for you to mull over, or, let's say, to contemplate. The main thing, the thing that really matters if we are to come to an agreement about the future of this novel—which is, I hope you understand, in my opinion, very fine, very, very fine—the main point is that there must be some movement. It's in the ending." He leaned back with his thick fingers tapping on his stomach. He squinted, then leaned forward again. "If you can change the ending, if you can move these characters toward a kind of resolution, an understanding of what their story has been about, I feel it is safe to say, I am confident in shaking your hand and saying, with a suitable new ending, that we have a deal."

With that, Mr Cole stood and extended his hand. I shook it. He smiled broadly, generously. He was old, benevolent Fezziwig from *A Christmas Carol,* that's who he was!

▼

Charlotte cannot be interrupted. She has been sitting all morning on a cushion in front of the fire, absorbed in a book called *Together Forever,* which is a biography of Chang and Eng, the original Siamese Twins.

They were not Siamese, in fact they were Chinese. But they were born in Siam in May, 1911. Their mother, a simple peasant woman, was completely bewildered by her peculiar issue, naturally, but, as mothers will, embraced them immediately and felt all the more loving and protective of them for their predicament. Neither peasant simplicity nor mother love prevented her, however, from being persuaded to sell them off at the age of twelve to an opportunistic Scottish businessman named Hunter, who later turned them over to show-business folks. Eventually, they found a home with P. T. Barnum.

Chang and Eng (Charlotte wonders why they were not called Eng and Chang) were apparently world-famous and much loved as entertainers and curiosities. They developed an act involving somersaults, little dance steps, recitations. They were clever with money, clear-headed and sure about their career and context. They travelled extensively. They were smart as whips, full of integrity, gentle, surprisingly easy-going men. Chang and Eng were attached at the chest only by a thick band of flesh which, in those days before X-rays, was a complete mystery: no one knew its function, its composition, and so they could not know the consequences of severing it. Throughout their lives, they explored every possibility of being surgically separated, consulting with the finest medical minds in many countries, but no doctor could in good conscience recommend the procedure.

Chang and Eng retired early and wealthy and moved to a farm in North Carolina. There they met and married two local sisters, Sarah and Adelaide. Of course, much was made in the community of these unions—everything from the snide insults and crude sexual references of the children to moral objections from religious and legal types. (Charlotte points out how interesting it is that in the face of greater problems, the issue of interracial marriage was never raised.)

I appreciate the general implications of their story, the depth of their circumstance and relationship, and am, of course, madly curious to know about their sex lives, which this book does not go into.

Charlotte just loves the delicious details. "Listen, you know, they fathered a whole bunch of kids. So, they kept two houses, close together. The arrangement was to spend three nights with Chang and his family and three nights with Eng and his. Each man's home was his castle, and when Chang stayed at Eng's or Eng stayed at Chang's, they were treated simply as guests. And did I tell you that if you touched one while they were sleeping, the other one woke up? And, also, they were allowed to ride on trains with only one ticket!" Their adjustments, the logistics of their daily lives intrigued and delighted Charlotte. While I was going over my marked-up manuscript at the kitchen table, I heard an alarming howl from Charlotte, and I went to her. She read aloud: " 'As they grew older, Chang became increasingly irritable,' " and we could not stop laughing.

But, it becomes a very sad story, actually. They were finally desperate to be separated, but they could not be. Chang drank heavily, destroying his temperament and physical health, while Eng was filled with anxiety watching the rapid decline of his other half. In 1874, Chang died of heart failure and, according to this book, Eng simply died of fright.

Charlotte had been gobbling up their story all morning, cackling with morbid amusement, fascinated, as she always is, with the extremes people can endure. But, just now, she came and stood in the kitchen doorway and said: "So, was it one life or two?"

And really, it is so complex. Who am I? And who am I? This question is life's project. Who am I in relation to you, when you are near, when I see you and touch you? Who am I, right now, this minute? Is it that I love you, or only that you have made some mark on me? Is it love, or merely that we are attached? Is it love that I've seen your motion and moods and can guess your next gesture, that I know you, that I will remember you?

Sometimes I think I am still struggling up that mountain of adolescent need and desire; and finally I'll reach the adulthood peak which will only confirm isolation, that I am alone. Charlotte's the one who has always thought about love. I can only collect these memories, and the stories from day to day. I'm like a witness. And if what I have is not exactly love, I know it is *something*.

▼

What I found this afternoon, no one would call garbage. It is one of those old-fashioned oil lamps with a sturdy brass base and a narrow glass chimney. It was wrapped in newspaper, set beside some discarded chairs and toys in front of the Turners'. Charlotte gets so irritated by my scavenging, but I don't see how she can object to this. I will pop into Hornstein's later to see if he sells lamp oil and wicks.

So, something has to happen to my characters. An event, a change.

A lesson.

Change. And stillness, quiet. The characters must move....Closer, or away? Away, I think, because people do move away. And that can be so sad.

Back to that old question, what is my novel about? Someone asks, what is your novel about? Togetherness, I answer.

Ten

Last night, a dream I've had many times. In the dream it is an orange dawn, and I am naked. I walk through the long corridor of our house, headed towards the kitchen, out onto the back porch. But my porch is gone. Replaced by an enormous, empty room, with a high, beamed ceiling and rows of ornate light fixtures. It's like the auditorium at our old school. Far at the end of this room is a small stage. Velvet curtains of a deep, dark green are closed. Somehow, I know they are going to open soon. There are no seats in the place, but I am anxious to wait and see what's behind the curtains. I am perfectly content to wait. I hear a thud coming from back stage. I hear a voice, then, singing, and say to myself: "That is a song I know." Which is when I awaken.

Charlotte loves this dream of mine. "It's so enchanting. And the whole point to it—I mean, the key to what this dream means—must be that you're naked."

This morning, I lay in bed, and the phone kept ringing. I was hoping, in vain, that Charlotte would pick it up. Finally, at the fifth ring I grabbed my robe, lunged from my room to the desk in the hall. It was Jesse. His voice was hoarse and weak. He asked me to meet him at the cafe in the city.

"Are you all right? You sound so strange," I said.

"Just come get me. Just come."

I told him it would take me some time, I wasn't dressed and the first train was not for another half hour. Jesse said: "As soon as you can. I'll be here."

I dressed hurriedly, and took a swallow of Charlotte's coffee. She was at the kitchen table; one of the tea cups from that old set of her mother's was in three sad pieces before her; she looked at the pieces, looked at a tube of glue, contemplating the challenge. "Am I mending this cup because I like it or need it?" she inquired seriously. "Or only out of nostalgia? I really hate nostalgia...."

I told her of Jesse's call as I was putting on my overcoat and hat. "It sounds like something is wrong," she said.

"I don't know. He just told me to come meet him."

"Some catastrophe, I bet," Charlotte said.

It was an overcast, still morning. In the city, I walked the few blocks from the train terminal to the cafe, and a cold drizzle began.

Jesse was inside, at a corner table. I headed towards him. He looked up at me.

"My God," I whispered, lowering myself onto the chair opposite him. He turned his face. He took both my hands in his and pressed with his fingers.

"Want some coffee?" he asked. He called to that cute young waiter who keeps dyeing his hair different colors: "Hey, can we get another coffee?"

Jesse looked directly at me then, and my eyes stayed with his, did not turn away. His right eye was swollen, nearly shut, surrounded by a huge dark grey bruise with a yellowish center. His bottom lip was swollen, too, and raw and moist. There were cuts, one very deep, on his chin.

After letting me have a long look at his beaten face, he said: "Wait, let me show you this," and he took a folded handkerchief from his shirt pocket. The handkerchief was spotted and smeared with brown blood stains. He set it on the table between us, pulled the corners aside to reveal two teeth, which rolled against each other and clicked softly. "Those are mine," Jesse said. "Those are *my* teeth." I thought he was going to cry.

My coffee came, and Jesse's was refilled. He took a few deep, purposeful breaths.

"You know," he began, "sometimes how you walk around and you just think something bad's about to happen? Well, sometimes that's what I think. And then I tell myself, hey, you're just a paranoid.

"I was out really late last night. Me and these friends of mine, Carla and Paul. Paul's an old boyfriend from a long time back, and now we're just good friends. And Carla's this woman from England who runs an art gallery. She had taken me and Paul to this party. Great party. It got kind of crazy, though, too crowded. So, finally, we said, let's go down to the Q Saloon, which is this gay bar, you know. I guess we all were a little bit punchy or something, but not really drunk, not loaded. We got a cab and we were sitting in the back of this cab, headed downtown and Carla says: 'Don't forget, boys'— and she's got this terrific English accent, right?—'it is a full moon tonight, and that means people can be terribly insane.' Which, me and Paul just laughed at, you know.

"Must have been like one-thirty in the morning by this time. The cab let us out at the corner. The bar's halfway down the block. Paul and I linked our arms over each other's shoulders and started walking, and Carla was right next to Paul, and we're headed towards the door of the Q Saloon. And then all of a sudden, really from out of nowhere, there's this shape in front of us. I mean, I must have been looking at the ground or something. Because this shape just appeared, and it took a second to focus, to see it was a man. Right in front of us. And then from either side comes two other guys, so there was a line of them in front of us, staring us down.

"I squinted to see them, and they were really young, like teenagers, and the first thing I thought was, this is nothing, they're just kids. So I smiled.

"One of these kids says: 'So you going to the fag bar?' I felt Paul really get stiff, tense. And after a couple of seconds, Carla said something like: 'Can we help you boys?'

"The three kids laughed then, which made it seem, I don't know, scarier or something. I had this impulse to take my arm from around Paul, but I couldn't move, really, I felt cornered.

"Carla says: 'What is this, anyway?' and just at that moment, there was this loud noise behind us, and all this activity. Paul and I separated, we turned around. And there were two more of these kids. They had come out of an alley and knocked over a garbage can.

"So, we were like surrounded by these kids. It was so dark. I had my back to those first three, and I turned around fast and one of them had a baseball bat.

"I mean, at this point, it was just this flurry of movements, and now when I remember it, it seems like it all happened in silence. But, it probably was really loud. I couldn't see Paul, I couldn't see Carla. I remember I kept looking over in the area of the bar, I was hoping to see some other person around, a car or something.

"All that was clear was these kids: a couple had leather jackets I think, and there were boots, blue jeans, a few caps maybe. And this damn baseball bat was swinging around. And different ones were shouting out 'Fag,' 'Queer,' 'Cocksucker,' stuff like that.

"Then two of these guys got a hold of me. One grabbed my arms behind my back and his friend started punching me in the stomach. I was doubled over, but trying to kick at them, trying to wriggle my way out.

"Then I heard Paul scream my name, which got me really desperate and panicked, because I thought those other ones were maybe killing him or something. I got just so scared about Paul. I really love Paul."

Jesse lit a cigarette. His arm was obviously hurting, he moved it so slowly, his hand was stiff and weak.

"The more I struggled, the worse it got and finally these two threw me on the curb, up against a parked car. They kicked. They took turns kicking me. I was saying to myself: Is this ever going to end? I was wondering if Carla had run for help, or was she just speechless in shock, or crying, or what? I mean, God, did they crack Paul's head open with a baseball bat?

"So, with every kick, this one guy, this one who seemed like he was the leader, kept saying: 'Fag, fag, fag, fag.' It was like a rhythm.

"As quick as this whole thing had started, it stopped. All of a sudden. Their footsteps running back up the alley and then no voices, no sounds. Except I could hear my own breathing. Then I heard Paul kind of crying, and I saw him, sitting all curled up by the garbage can, and looking at him made me sad and shocked and terrified, and I guess when he saw me, he kind of got more upset. When we each saw how bad the other one had been beaten, that's what did it, we moved towards each other and just were bawling.

"It was like a trauma. Like being tortured by terrorists or something. Like being victims, you know, someone's helpless victim, I mean, it was unbelievable.

"We made it into the bar, and Carla was in there already, she came rushing up and told us she'd called the police. There were ten or fifteen guys in the place, all dead quiet, just staring at us.

"Police took a while to get there. They came in wearing these masks and rubber gloves, you know how they do, they're afraid they'll catch

AIDS or whatever.

"Me and Paul rode with them to the station. They took pictures of us. I asked the captain or whoever he was: 'Are we being booked for something?' He was pretty nice. He said they just wanted photographic evidence of our injuries.

"Then they put us in this square room with a table and gave us cigarettes and coffee. Which is funny because Paul had this big thing about how he had quit smoking and quit drinking coffee, but I guess he just didn't care. After a while two detectives and this woman social worker came in and they took statements from us about the whole incident. Descriptions of the kids, which we weren't too good at. We signed the papers and they let us go.

"Paul was really sad. I was feeling angry by this time, but Paul just looked sad, very lonely and quiet.

"I was exhausted, I was so tired, the whole time I just wanted to get in my bed and sleep for the whole day. But then when we left the station this morning I couldn't bring myself to go home for some reason. I came here, called you."

Jesse said nothing more; he did not look at me but at the cigarette between his fingers.

"How does your face feel?"

"My face? Oh, my face feels okay. My arm's sore. My hand is pretty achy. Legs hurt a lot, because they were mostly kicking my legs."

"I think you should go home and take a bath. I'll come with you if you want. Want me to come with you and help you take a bath, get you in bed?"

Jesse stood. "No, no, that's nice and stuff, but I think I'm okay. No, I've got a couple of things to do, and then I'll head on home."

I rose. I touched his shoulder. "Jesse, you don't seem in good shape. You seem distracted. Don't you want someone to be with you, at least for an hour or so?"

"What? No, no, I don't think I need that. I think I'm pretty much okay, just banged up and everything." He pulled a couple of crinkled dollar bills from his pants pocket and dropped them on the table. "Here, let me get the coffee for you. I mean, thanks a lot for coming to meet me and everything. I mean, yeah, thanks. And I'll give you a call." Jesse turned and walked out the side entrance of the cafe. I remained at our table, bewildered, holding my breath. I put the handkerchief and those two teeth of Jesse's in my coat pocket.

On the train home, I had the whole smoking car to myself. I sat in a serious, almost frenzied contemplation of the terrible story I'd just heard. How could it happen? What formed and motivated the boys? What does it mean? But, I could not know these answers, and the attempt to organize something rational and comprehensible was only a way to slide through terror.

My real consideration, I suppose, was that it might have been me. My eye could be bruised, my lip swollen, my teeth wrapped in a handkerchief.

What an enormous amount we live through, and must accept, only to survive. Charlotte tries to teach me this truth. But I need a better teacher, I think. A teacher with adequate perspective, who can show me more than her own scars.

Teacher, why is there so much pain and struggle? If it is ultimately important or necessary, tell me. Explain the number burned on Hornstein's arm and the results of my next blood tests and that tragic little Turner girl and beautiful Jesse's broken face. Teacher, *I* do not stay locked inside my house. I cannot, as Charlotte can, find refuge in the same old books, year after year, the same private and protected occupations. I go out, and am confronted by the desperate people, sick people, and a thousand kinds of monster: greedy, slick, brutal, brilliant, hopeless. I try my best to stay amused and cool and easy, while being forced to witness humanity.

Charlotte knows what a big, bad world it is. Charlotte knows it's not safe even to be safe. However, I have no valiant, certain conclusions about life, except that there is pain. Teacher, if you can show me anything, show me how to care.

94

Spring

Eleven

That April morning, the neighborhood smelled of sausage and syrup and wet leaves. I was sitting on the back porch, wrapped in two sweaters and an afghan, holding a cup of steaming tea. I had O. Henry's short stories open on my lap. The sick little Turner girl was in the yard, dragging a stick through frozen dirt. Charlotte tells me the girl's name is Rose.

Monday, my complaint was only a dry cough—incomplete, unsatisfying. That night was sleepless, and I woke with a fever, my pyjamas damp from sweat. The next couple of days, I had energy enough only to get from my bed to the back porch, and even with that small effort, my breathing was labored. Charlotte would cheerily bring me an enormous glass of orange juice, and tell me not to smoke too much, and then go on with her newest project—a sloppy collage made with newspaper photos of criminals and police.

By Thursday, I knew I was getting weaker, that I truly was sick. I began to panic. I wanted counsel, I wanted my condition to be taken seriously and attended to, and finally I asked Charlotte: "Do you think I ought to call Dr Decker?"

"Well, if it gets much worse, if you don't seem to be improving, then maybe give him a call. But, you really look better to me today. There's color in your cheeks." A bit of Charlotte's hair was crusted with paste; her huge, sincere black eyes blinked at me. She fixed her vodka and tea mixture in a giant jelly jar. She has been drinking more lately.

But I was not getting better—a continuing fever, the fatigue—and I began to realise that, with this illness, I was alone. Charlotte could not take care of me, other than in the most abstract sort of way, only by her presence, by being herself; she could never protect or rescue me. Charlotte has always been my guide, walking a few steps ahead and glancing back; but if I fall really far behind, if I am trying to call to her but cannot get my breath, will she turn around?

Friday evening, Charlotte ran a bath for me, but it was lukewarm. I adjusted it to suit me and sat for a quarter of an hour, trying to relax. I heard the phone; I counted nine rings. Charlotte cannot always be relied upon to answer the phone. And as I was draining the bath, I saw a strange bruise on my knee, a raised spot, violet-colored. I stared at this blemish, holding my breath, remembering.

The spring I was fifteen. I was walking down by the railroad tracks after supper, tossing stones. The sky was pale orange in the west and darkened, deepened to sapphire-blue in the east; the air was still and warm. I came upon the Travelers Inn, a dilapidated, ancient bar near the river. (Today, it is boarded up.) A man was sitting in a red car with the door open, drinking beer from a bottle, and he called me over. He wanted to know if I liked beer, and I said I'd never tried it. He gave me a sip. He said: "Hop on in," and I slipped onto the passenger seat.

He was young, in his early twenties. He had thick lips and a long, straight nose. His hair fell over his collar. His shirt was vulgar, turquoise and yellow, made of some synthetic material. He remarked how hot it was and stroked his chest with his hand. He said he was a singer, pointed to a guitar in the back of his car. The red neon sign—TRAVELERS—flashed a rhythm, illuminating his smooth face, his neck. He told me he was driving across the country, on his way to Texas to perform in nightclubs.

He put his fingers on my thigh and squeezed. Finally, he said: "Let me see that," and undid my trousers. An eager little white pole stuck out, skinny and hard. He bent over my lap and took it in his mouth. My shoulders shot up, my head leaned back, I swallowed hard. Two seconds, and I was finished. My spine twitched, I collapsed. The man took a gulp of beer, sloshed it around in his mouth, and then spat on the gravel.

I ran up the hill, panting. Charlotte was behind her father's tool shed, sneaking a smoke. I told her every detail, every word that had been exchanged, all the nuances which revealed the scope. Charlotte, I remember, was curious mostly about the character of my partner—had he any other kind of sex life, or did he just lure boys into his car on spring evenings; had he ever been arrested; was he actually a pervert?

It was about a week later that I woke one morning to find a red bump on my penis. I panicked. I trudged through school profoundly depressed that day, raced into the boys' room every hour or so to stare and touch and squeeze, and the bump was only getting bigger, discoloring.

I could not even turn to Charlotte about this. I couldn't eat supper. My mother said: "What *is* the matter with you?" and I said: "Nothing, nothing, all right? Can't a person have things on his mind?" Which astounded my parents.

The next morning when this deformity was still present, I decided to take action. I looked up syphilis and gonorrhea in a book on a top shelf in my father's study; I breathed rapidly and crooked, hot lines of sweat shot down my temples to my jaw as I read of the wreckage and heartache these diseases cause.

Finally, I searched through the phone book under Medical and Social Services and found the number for the city's V.D. Clinic. I dialed, hung up, dialed again. "Yes, I was wondering, if someone has a spot on his penis, like sort of like a pimple, what could that be?" The woman at the V.D. Clinic said it might just be a pimple. She asked if I'd had any sexual contact. I lied and said no. She said it could be any number of things, or nothing at all, and it would be best to come into the clinic and get examined. We hung up before I got the chance to ask: Will I die? Is this something horrible, that I'll die from? What about blindness? And you can lose your mind, I had heard.

I prayed. Please make this go away. Please make this disappear. I'll never, and I'm sorry, and I promise.... If only this will please, *please,* go away.

I dared to pray. I did not ask for forgiveness or even guidance. I prayed for grace, for the gift of rescue.

The little bump was gone within a day or two. How well I remember the panic, the desperation, but I've no memory of any relief or gratitude at being finally delivered from the humiliating, disgusting fate I had imagined.

So, sitting on the edge of the tub, prodding at the lesion on my knee, my newest blemish, the fear was familiar. This mark measures time and secrets, connects me today with that frightened, excited, naughty, guilty, ignorant child. Another dot on my skin, all these years later, challenging me to accept it for what it is, forfeit my guessing and the hopeless bargaining with this God so soundly rejected by Charlotte and me.

The neighborhood was shot with streaks from the sun, with cold. The Turner woman called Rose inside for breakfast; the girl pretended not to have heard the summons, and then got scolded and stomped her way up their back steps. I smiled.

I smiled, and surrender was coming, with an ache of tears behind my eyes. Charlotte was busy in the kitchen, burning our English muffins, and I knew that I was sick now and had to go to the hospital. Maybe I was thinking it was my last morning on my beloved back porch. Those geraniums should be re-potted; and when was the last time the window was washed? Maybe I was frightened of slick floors and white uniforms and people prone on tables being wheeled through corridors. When I am gone from here, I was thinking...when I am gone from here....And I was not remembering even from one thought to the next, I who normally live in this easy, sweet play of memory.

"Charlotte?"

She stepped onto the porch wearing an oven mitt on each hand.

"I want you to feel my forehead," I said.

It seemed a long moment, a queer pause, and I even thought she might refuse. But, she took off one of the bulky mitts and put her palm against my head. "Yes," she said, frowning. "Yes, you are very warm." Like it was a contest and she had lost.

▼

I'm sure I always will remember that early morning, the shaky walk down the front steps of our house. Though spring was fresh and scented and warm, I wore my winter coat, two scarves, mis-matched mittens and a knit cap pulled over my ears. Charlotte was barely visible, standing in the dark corridor, her arms folded across her chest, watching through the doorway.

Ahead of me was Mr Hornstein's handsome son, David, standing beside the open door on the passenger side of his truck. There were faces in the windows of the Turner house. So, all these eyes followed my long, troubled journey, and I was unsure if I would ever return. Too unsure to say goodbye to Charlotte, too unsure to cry.

David said: "I put a bunch of newspapers on the seat, make it more comfortable," and he grasped my elbow, helped me into the truck.

"I'm all right," I said.

He drove slowly through our dead town and eased onto the two-lane highway that would take us into the city.

"It's nice of you to drive me," I said to David.

"Oh, that's no problem, no problem. Listen, are you warm enough?"

"Yes, really, I'm fine. We called my doctor and he just said he thought it was a good idea for me to check into the hospital for some tests."

David tapped his horn at a red compact car which was moving too slow, and then he passed it. "You have to go to the doctor's a lot, don't you?"

"Yes, pretty often. Yes, I do."

We had to talk loud, nearly shouting, to be heard over the clattering, chugging truck. We were passing a ravaged, weathered old barn Charlotte and I have always loved so much; it is wooden, has not been painted in my lifetime, it seems to be just barely standing, but still it is a majestic structure. And we passed that Catholic convent and the school.

"I've always thought it was pretty wonderful how you are with Charlotte," David said. He faced forward as he drove, kept his chin up.

"How do you mean?"

"You seem very loyal to her. You've really stuck by her."

He must have shaved just that morning, because there were two tiny pink blood dots on his throat.

"She was always a strange girl, wasn't she? Kind of the eccentric type." David smiled. "And the guys would say things about her, the girls, too. But, I always liked her. I wondered about Charlotte a lot."

I was trying to recall David Hornstein and his many dazzling friends from our school days. Here beside him, for one second I had a sense of being protected.

"You two were pretty much always best friends, weren't you? God, I had a best friend back then, but I don't know where he is now. Everybody moved away. Everybody got all caught up in college and marriage and careers."

Healthier, not so weak, I would have interrogated strapping David Hornstein—why didn't you get married? What brought you back home? But I didn't need to. He drove slow and talked to me.

101

"A lot of times I thought I was gay. I had a few experiences, you know. It was all right with guys. I mean, it wasn't any better or any worse than with girls. Maybe I'm bi-sexual or something. Maybe everyone deep down is bi-sexual. I just think I don't have much interest in sex at all."

David stopped the truck behind a line of cars, backed up due to road work. For another few minutes we proceeded so slowly our movement was imperceptible. "Time really runs by, doesn't it? Next thing I know, it's a whole other decade. I'm remembering things that seem just like last week, but they were years and years ago. Do you know what I mean?"

And then that familiar vista, the city emerging in a pulsing glow; we leave behind rocks and dirt and crooked town buildings and enter this real life. In the city, when fire trucks are called it is to manage a huge, threatening blaze. There is tragedy and heroism; not, as at home, a dusty, casual resignation to false alarms....

"I used to kind of race around," David went on. "I did some fairly wild stuff at one time. Drank a lot. And, after high school, after I left home, it seemed like I spent half my time in bed with someone. People thought I was a pretty goodlooking kid, you know. So, maybe I used up all my energy, being crazy way back then. Maybe I had my share of excitement."

We were slowed down once again, a minor accident. No one seemed hurt, but two bald men were standing at the side of the road, each beside a white car, like twins, staring, perplexed, at their bumpers. It was a comical picture; but all of me ached—my jaw, my joints, to swallow and to cough—so I saw it indistinctly, and then we had passed.

"Because now I feel just fine staying home. Do my work around the store for my dad. A movie once in a while. And I like to read. You're a big intellectual type, aren't you? Well, I like reading. I'm thinking maybe I'll start writing some poetry."

We pulled onto the major city thoroughfare and, ahead, I could see the tan brick buildings of the hospital complex. I was getting scared now, and overheated. I dreaded being left alone at the hospital and wondered if David Hornstein would come inside with me.

"Anyway," he said, sighing, "it's good the way you stay with Charlotte and take care of her. She's had lots of problems in her life. And she's got a good friend in you."

As it turned out, David did not leave me. He helped me inside, through the emergency entrance and stood with me at the desk as I filled out the admission papers. We sat together, waiting, and then an orderly came with a wheelchair to take me to the ward.

David smiled—the expression was charitable, but distant, and those enormous grey eyes of his never look anything but sad—and squeezed my shoulder. "You're going to be fine," he said. He watched me being rolled down the slick corridor. I'm sure he was not too offended that I could not say thank you. I think he must have understood.

▼

My first day at the hospital was filled with taking tests and sleeping, and I woke the following morning lost and confused in this bright white room. "Oh, Jesus," I heard from behind the curtain separating the two beds. "I was so worried about her. Thanks so much for taking care of her. Okay, then. Call me later." The curtain was pulled back sharply. The young man sitting in the center of the bed across from me blinked and grinned. He had curly, paper-white hair and astonishingly pale skin. He was skinny, brittle, with a head that looked like it was barely balanced on the stick neck and bony shoulders; I thought of a ventriloquist's dummy. "Hope I didn't wake you?" he asked. "I was trying to be real quiet?" He had that unnerving brand of Southern drawl which ends each sentence in a question mark, a lift in intonation. I tried to smile. Round his side of the room, Get Well cards were taped to the walls, and there were stuffed animals in the chair, and flowers. "I've been so worried about my cat Zsa Zsa? That was my upstairs neighbor on the phone? She says Zsa Zsa's fine?"

This was Sandy. He's been sick for a year, in and out of this hospital. He knows all the nurses, and entertains them. He spends much of his time on the phone. Sandy is a member of an organization called, I think, Round-Up, a square dancing club for gay men. So, he has been visited by several fellows wearing cowboy hats and boots, bolo ties and beards, handsome, humorous comrades; they all call each other 'honey,' and enjoy themselves tremendously.

His parents, Mildred and Earl, have visited every day. She is compact

103

and stern and anxious, keeps a pocketbook always under her arm or on her lap; he is tall and plump, with a red face and thinning blond hair and a huge, friendly smile, his shirt tail just about to come undone.

There's an infuriatingly cheerful nurse who hooked me up to a computer and made me breathe through a tube, then had me walk on a conveyor belt which she slowly tilted, to simulate trekking up a hill. To see if I got tired. I did.

Charlotte has called me, several times a day. Of course, she will not be able to come visit, the idea has not even been considered. Dr Decker had a long talk with me, explaining my diagnosis, and I phoned to tell Charlotte. I have pneumocystis carinii, which is a rare and problematical form of pneumonia; it is serious, it is sometimes fatal. Also, I have Kaposi's Sarcoma, a cancer, the cause of that lesion on my knee. These infections are common to people with AIDS, I told her. Charlotte said: "Well, my sister will be coming to see you. She's going to bring you some fruit. And I've been reading this most amazing book about American history, all the strange little facts we aren't taught in grammar school, it's fascinating. So, Annie will bring that for you, too." And in other phone calls, she is delighted and captivated by my descriptions of the nurses, how I sneak down the corridor for a cigarette, and she especially likes to hear of Sandy and his gay cowboy friends. It is understood, though, in that same way we understand so much with each other, that any discussion of illness or death is unacceptable.

▼

As I was being wheeled on a gurney through the white and green corridor, I focused my eyes on my own bare toes. I tried to breathe steadily. I am being peacefill, I kept telling myself. I am being peaceful.

My cart was pushed against a wall and a nurse said: "Be right back. Don't move now."

I am being peaceful.

Whatever the drugs were, they were taking over. A door to the left of me was pushed open urgently and a foursome— two men, two women, all in white coats with stethoscopes round their necks—breezed quickly past. One of the women, the apparent leader, walked ahead of the others and talked over her shoulder about equipment and blood and units. The other three, medical students perhaps, followed close at her heels, nodding vigorously, absorbing her descant. After some moments, the same group again marched by me; this time each one was eating a doughnut from the cafeteria.

I was rescued then, wheeled through sets of doors which closed and opened softly, silently, like curtains. My eyelids, by now, had minds of their own and would not stay open. I was stood up against the X-ray screen, held there with my arms at different angles, told to hold my breath, let it out, hold it, let it out. I am being peaceful, I am being peaceful.

Someone bathed me with a thick, soft cloth, and I was too tired and drugged to feel discomfited by the invasion. Delirium had turned my fear into something thin, pointless.

The moment I was helped into bed, I drifted to sleep, despite Sandy's chattering on the phone. "He said *what?*" I heard. "Well, that's a bald-faced lie? You know, he's just that jealous type?"

That sleep was not just sleep, and it gave me my most vivid dream. I am in the backyard. The flowers are all blue. The sky is a solid lavender-colored dome. I am leaning against a motorcycle, one of those shiny black, old-fashioned ones. Then Charlotte calls me. I look all around, do not see her. "Here! Up here!" She is sitting up high in the willow tree, in a V of the trunk, peering through the loose, hanging branches.

"I'm going to go for a ride," I tell her. I am angry, but I don't know why.

"That will be fun, that will be wonderful."

"Charlotte, why don't you come with me?"

"No, no, no, no, no," and she is singing this word sweetly to a fanciful tune.

"Charlotte, you don't want to see me ride off, do you? You don't want me to go away, forever, to just disappear?"

Then I woke up. Pitiless headache, travelling down my neck to my shoulders. I have not told Charlotte this dream. Of course, I am dissecting its dialogue and images, prospecting for meaning. Well, it's something about abandonment, I can see. But, who is leaving whom? I take a ride on a magnificent black machine—toward what? for how long?— and it seems it is a hostile action. I'm mad, I guess. Because she would let me go.

Twelve

Annie did come visit. She was reserved, but tender, too, and I was pleased to see her. She sat on the edge of my bed, her fur coat across her lap, peering suspiciously and disapprovingly, but discreetly, at Sandy and his parents. Annie told me about a friend of hers who has AIDS, has lived with it for some time, and that these illnesses associated with AIDS are not automatically a death sentence as they were a few years ago. I appreciated this reassurance. But Annie seemed hurried and distant, and finally I said: "Don't let me keep you, Annie, thanks for stopping by, thanks for the gifts."

"It's just that I have to catch that train." She kissed my forehead. I realised, then, that Annie has been staying with Charlotte while I've been in the hospital. Charlotte cannot stay alone, of course.

A nice, nervous call from Mr Cole. And a card from Mr Hornstein. A sloppy note arrived from Henry Beale who now lives at a commune in New Mexico.

Jesse came for a visit. His face is completely healed now, and he looks his old self: dirty and healthy and young. He was grumpy, though; he fidgeted with some hospital rubber gloves, pumped the blood pressure machine, went into the bathroom two or three times. Perhaps he was stoned on all of his little pills.

We watched a television preacher, Reverend Bill, for a few minutes. Reverend Bill was curing people over the airwaves. Reverend Bill sensed that someone in his audience was suffering with a tipped pelvis, and someone else with a crooked spine and, with his eyes closed, he urged us all to place a hand on our television screens. This I cannot do as the set is perched high on the wall at the corner. "There's a brain tumor out there. *Heal.*" He sensed an unbalanced uterus. *Heal.* Praise God! "I know," Reverend Bill reflected, "I know maybe some of you, maybe your ills have not been called out today. Well, let me tell you what you do. What you do, what you do is just start praising God."

I was confounded into silence by this dubious performance. But, Jesse said: "What shit."

I put on my robe and we walked down the corridor to the smoking lounge. I was tired. I was glad to see Jesse, glad he had thought to come, but we didn't have much to say.

We sat in yellow plastic chairs. There's a little radio in the lounge and I turned it on.

"Sure is a depressing place," said Jesse. "This ward, I mean. This is a special AIDS ward, isn't it?"

"Yes, yes it is."

Silence, then: "I know for a fact that I won't get AIDS."

I drew on my cigarette, pulled open the window blind a bit.

"It's something a person creates for himself. If you don't let sickness into your thoughts, you won't, you know, get it."

The Mills Brothers on the radio: *Nevertheless.* Charlotte adores the old Mills Brothers records. In our front room, she sometimes sings along, mimicking their splendid harmony, and she dances in a fluid circle, waving around a cigarette, wearing dark glasses.

"Yes, people say that sort of thing," I answered Jesse. "I don't know. Do you think I brought this on myself?"

He moved forward in his seat, his response was quick. 'Well, I'm not saying that. I don't say that about you. All I'm saying is, for myself, I will not allow the thoughts, the possibility. I won't let myself get sick."

"Do you have safe sex, though?" I asked him.

"Do I? I do what feels right to me at any given time." His look was defiant. "I don't worry about being safe or being unsafe or anything like that. I do what...what I need to do."

Jesse was sullen, then. Maybe he thought I was angry. I wasn't. I was thinking about that guy Terry—or was his name Willie?—that guy who used to be cute and then got so sick. Has he died?

Strange about the choices people make. Mine have not propelled me toward great success or fulfillment. I have not pursued mating, intimacy and commitment, but rather sought sexual adventure, intrigue, variety. I have hoped for friendship. I have clung to my passivity.

There is some truth in Jesse's philosophy, there is some choice we have in the creation of our lives. I suppose if I had really wanted money, I'd have gone after it, and fame and respectability. Generally, the people who have it all are the people who wanted it all.

One constant conscious desire has been to write. This enterprise has been my romance, my accomplishment, my fantasy, my chore. I will never understand—and I'm sure I'll always feel some regret—why the energy I've had for hearing and telling stories was never able to be channeled into insurance sales, or real estate, or medicine, law, politics. Writing is a nice enough talent to possess, but making up stories is really a closed passage, not much of a career. Perhaps I should write sermons.

I have not chosen to be ill, I don't think, but in a curious way I have decided to spend my time wishing I lived some other place, had some other life. Always just slightly discontented, searching for safety, and remembering. And always to return to the quiet and familiarity of Charlotte; I have found comfort in her steadiness, her selective certainty. Choosing this queer life with her I have chosen, at least, not to be alone.

▼

My condition has improved. Dr Decker has told me I will only be here for a few days, that my infection was caught early, nothing too serious. Obviously, though, this hospital stay represents more than a broken leg. It admits that I am terminal, confirms that my system is bent, broken, cracked. Everyone keeps saying Get Well. Except Charlotte. Charlotte will say no such thing—she assumes that I *am* getting well, that I will *of course* get well.

This morning I caught a look at my shadow on the cream-colored hospital wall—astonishing. It's like some grotesque distortion. The neck is long and thin, the hair is wispy and sticks out at the top of my head, the ears seem enormous and oddly shaped. Then I lifted up my hands: the fingers are long slender strings with knots in them, attached to delicate skinny wrists. It is part of a process which they call the "wasting syndrome." Charlotte thinks that a vulgar title, but romantic: "It's like when people used to have consumption," she said, "and they'd go to these marvelous spas in Switzerland."

This Sandy character, even stuck in bed, is so lively and winsome

108

and active. He told me he celebrated his twenty-fourth birthday a week before being admitted to the hospital. And he is desperate to go back to his favorite bar. "All my friends have sent me cards? They're just all dying for me to come on home?" He has told me all about his two lovers; they form an equal triangle and have been together six months. Both men are named Roger. "I call them Roger One and Roger Two?" he explained with a thoroughly winning laugh.

He changes the television channel with the remote control every few minutes, searching for his favorite game shows, and keeps talking. "She's a housewife," says Sandy, referring to the champion. Regarding the challenger: "He's in computer school? God, he's kind of cute?" Music swells, the studio audience gets frenzied, and Sandy plays along vigorously. "Go for it, go! Take the two hundred! Oh, what a jerk? Okay. Let's see what category this jerk will pick? Okay, world cities? Okay. What? *Vienna?* It's Buenos Aires, jerk."

With Sandy's parents visiting so frequently, memories of my own parents have surfaced, flickering familiar pictures for me to squint at. My mother has been dead twelve years. She was on her way to Florida, to see her retired brother, and the plane crashed. Charlotte whispered: "God, I just knew that plane would crash, I sensed it."

The strange thing is I've always believed my mother sensed it, too. I accompanied her to the airport. The departure was delayed an hour. My mother seemed anxious and irritated. She sent me to the airport bar and had me bring her a scotch and water—a rare thing for her—and we sat silently. People played cards, using their luggage as tables, and children exhausted themselves chasing each other round pillars, into and out of bathrooms. It grew darker. I tried to read a paperback mystery, but could not concentrate. And my mother, holding tight to a pink and white flight bag on her lap, said: "I just don't like this," softly, not to me really, not to anyone, but in an accusing way.

Finally, boarding was announced, and the passengers grabbed purses and bags and their cranky children and formed an uneven, miserable line, and my mother blended in. I saw her broad shoulders move with the crowd, and she smiled graciously as she handed her ticket to an attendant. She was always polite. My mother believed in being polite. And she disappeared down a ramp.

I raced through the airport to my car, across an empty night-time freeway. I had a date that night.

My father lives in New England now, teaching at a boy's prep school. He's got a new wife, Julia. She was a militant feminist when they met, but now she is a gourmet cook. She's always sweet to me, sends me cards for my birthday. My father, though, does not call or write. He objects to my homosexuality.

It was on a visit several years ago that I told him I was gay. We sat on a dismal powder-blue sofa in his new living room. Julia had put cute cartoon coasters on every table-top.

Dad wanted to know what I meant by gay, he challenged me. He went on, a little too forcefully I thought, about the word 'gay' being usurped and distorted, that it used to be a perfectly fine word, meaning merriment and happiness, and now it's been destroyed. Whatever has developed and changed in the world since World War II is thoroughly confounding and a bit distasteful to my father.

I said: "Well, whatever you want to call it, then."

He asked: "Have you ever actually tried it?"

"Yes," I answered. "I've tried it."

He told me it was something he simply could not live with. And I always wonder, is it really that? Because, I have found, over the years since, that there are qualities and parts of his life that I cannot live with either: Julia, New England, the beard he has grown, the pipe he smokes. I do not like to see him paunchy and limited, settled into powder-blue cushions; I am serene with an old memory of him in his armchair, relaxed, a bit distant, so much bigger than I, and do not wish for any other kind of father. So, perhaps he remembers me in my cowboy costume, or reading giant picture books, or asking important questions with scraped elbows and constant nightmares, and as the only child of that woman who died in a plane crash; and he does not wish for any other kind of son.

▼

Woke at dawn and, in the dimness, scribbled down this dream: I find myself walking through a pine forest. The coolest possible place. The floor is a surface of brown and grey pine needles, so soft I bounce as

I walk. I'm dressed in my thin hospital smock, open at the back. I am smiling. I come to a clearing. Then a wall of wet rocks and, below that, a large pond, slowly moving towards a waterfall, carrying leaves and twigs... moving green.... So, I leap into this pond, splash about, dunk my head. Shed my smock, wheel around, so light in water, in ecstasy which I have never known or imagined in my waking life, which I *felt*. The sensation in this dream, opposed to all I know of sensation, was one of perfect health. Finally I wiggled my way to a shadowed declivity in the rocks, and as I climbed out of the pond, I awoke, in tears.

Thirteen

Sunday I was discharged from the hospital. I waited all morning for Dr Decker to sign the papers. I was dressed, my little bag was packed. David Hornstein was to pick me up and drive me home, but he'd not yet arrived. I was irritated and getting restless, still weak from having moved so little these past few days. I stepped into the smoking lounge. The radio was turned to a classical station. I sat in a chair next to a potted plant and looked out the window: silver fog had settled over the parking lot, muting all colors, and I felt sadness, exhausted at the mere thought of my coming recuperation.

Earl, Sandy's father, walked in and settled his enormous, sloppy frame into the chair across from me. He lit a cigarette and nodded to me, ran his fingers through those few strands of blond hair. "You getting out today?"

"Yes. Yes, finally."

He put the palms of his hands against his temples and pressed hard.

"Are you all right, sir?" I asked, and there was no response. I still call people's fathers 'sir.' "Is it Sandy? I was under the impression Sandy was doing all right...."

Earl looked at me. His eyes were moist. "Sandy? Oh, Sandy's a whole lot better. Sandy....No, it isn't Sandy. Thank God. It's something else. It's a certain situation I got myself into." He paused. "I'm...in trouble." We looked at each other and Earl whispered: "Can I speak to you? It's a confidential matter."

"Of course."

"Here's the story, then. You've met my wife. Mildred?"

I nodded.

"Mildred and I are married now twenty-nine years. We met in school. Mildred worked for a few years and then we decided to have our family, we had our daughter Susan, and then Sandy. Mildred wasn't much interested in a career. We live in a pretty small town, a Southern town. Good place for children. We've been in that house for eighteen years. I'm in publishing. Textbooks. Mathematics textbooks. Maybe I'm not making sense. The point is, it's a secure life. We've built this life for ourselves, together." Earl's speech was a pleasant, slow drawl, not so grating as his son's; not as lively either. He lit a cigarette, sniffled and went on.

"So, it was just seven months ago. It seems like years. I met this young woman. April. She's a new editor at another company in my building. I was attracted right away. She was real bright, real enthusiastic.

"I can't even remember how it all got started. We just flirted with each other a lot. Then, we went out for a couple of drinks. April loves all the old movies and so do I."

"So do I, Earl," I interjected.

Earl smiled tightly, nervously. "So, anyway, we talked about our favorites, you know. We got to laughing about different things. It felt very nice. Nice. To be laughing." Through the window I saw a flock of pigeons make a broad circle and soar away.

Earl coughed and continued: "So, we began this affair. Which is funny, because I never had any kind of affair before. I never even had sex with any woman other than Mildred. And I was thinking...I don't know... that it was natural? That there was no harm to it? Somehow it seemed I was entitled. Like I had a right, sort of. To touch another person. To feel something different. And I would not want to hurt Mildred. Absolutely not. And absolutely I would never *leave* her. I didn't want to change my life, my home or family. I just wanted to shake things up a little, I guess.

"For me it was an adventure. It's embarrassing, now. I'm ashamed to be so...I don't know...so typical.

"But, I didn't promise anything to April, nothing. And I felt pretty safe with April because she seemed so independent in her life. If anything, it seemed like I was a little lovesick and April was more the aloof one.

"We went together a couple of nights a week, to April's apartment in the city. I would tell Mildred I had a meeting.

"My feelings for Mildred—I mean, it didn't make me lose my feelings for Mildred, far from it. In fact, I found myself real happy when we were together. I took Mildred out to shows and dinner, and we had some

113

wonderful, cozy nights. Our intimate relations, you know what I mean, it really got more frequent, more exciting. It was like I was rejuvenated. So, I told myself, this business with April is actually *good.* for my marriage. That's crazy, isn't it? I told myself that having an affair with April was really *helping* Mildred.

"Then, one afternoon, ten days ago, April phoned and said I should come to her apartment. I got worried. I thought she might be ill. And the first thing I noticed when I had gotten inside and taken off my coat was a photograph in a frame. Of me. I said, 'Where did you get that photograph?' She told me she'd seen portrait proofs I'd had done and she'd taken one from my briefcase. Which, I'll tell you, made me plenty uncomfortable, confused. She was in her bathrobe. Her hair was tied up. She was chain-smoking.

"And then began this talk, this strange, strange talk. She wanted to know what we were going to do. I didn't know what she meant, at first. 'Don't you think it's time we make some decisions?' she asks. She says, 'We should start talking about the future of our relationship.' So, I said, Well, I like you very much, I respect you, April.' I mean, I thought she was breaking the whole thing off, and I was going to be a gentleman about it, I wasn't going to argue. 'But,' she said, What about your wife?' My wife? My *wife?* She says, 'Do you intend to tell your wife about us?'

"And, you see, Sandy lives out here and he had just gotten sick again, he'd just been put in the hospital. I told April that, I said, We're having some difficulties right now, our son is real ill and my wife is under so much pressure.' And then I said—and this must have been the fatal blow—I said, "There really is no reason to involve my wife, to say anything to her.' I said, 'April, let's just end our romance. Let's be friends,' I said.

"'Friends?' She was practically hysterical, yelling. And then she started laughing. 'What do you mean by friends?' So, I said, 'Well, listen, our relationship is *not* going to go any further than it already has.' I was being firm with her, and honest. I said, 'I'm *not* going to divorce my wife and marry you.' So, April says, Why not?'

"And then she was walking around her apartment in circles, smoking like crazy. She's saying, 'I can't believe it, you're breaking up with me, after all of this,' she's saying. And I was getting panicked. I asked her what she had expected. I mean, what is it she expected, for God's sake? She said she thought we were in love. I said, 'Are you really in love with me, April, really?' But, she didn't answer. She didn't say she was in love with me. She just said, Well, aren't you in love with *me?*

"And here I was, and it was hitting me: I didn't really even *know* April. We were very different, we saw things very different. I flashed back to our first meeting, the way she acted, really in control, and I felt like now I was watching her come apart at the seams. Sinking. I was scared, because maybe she was taking me down with her.

"So, I tried to put an end to it. 'April,' I said, 'let's speak in a couple of days. Let's just get some perspective.' She wouldn't look at me, she was facing the window. And I left. I drove home, clutching the steering wheel, grinding my teeth. I was thinking, Oh, my God, what if this girl kills herself, what if she does something desperate?

"Over the week and a half before we came out to see Sandy, I got up to a dozen phone calls a day from April, and two letters sent to my office. She's sick, she's a sick young woman. She's determined to tell my wife." Earl curled his big paws into fists and put them to his mouth. His shoulders shook, his face got even redder. "Oh, Mildred. She's going to tell Mildred about our affair. And I've begged April, I've pleaded, Why do you want to do this to me? How will this benefit you? What do you think you will get by ruining my marriage, destroying the woman I adore?"

Earl was silent for a few moments, and calmer. We each lit cigarettes. I could hear a couple of nurses talking at the front desk.

I asked: "So, you are afraid this April will tell your wife?"

Earl nodded.

"Wouldn't it be best then if you told your wife? I mean, tell her yourself."

Earl let out a frustrated sigh. "It'll kill her. It'll break her spirit. And now, now with Sandy sick in the hospital. She's being so strong, she's trying so hard. And to find out about this...meaningless...meaningless... stupid affair with this crazy woman."

Earl whispered: "Maybe Mildred will ask me to move out. Oh, God. I know she'll hate me. I just couldn't stand it if she hated me."

What a queer subject, faithfulness. It is foreign to me, it does not come up. There never has been any question of my devotion or commitment to Charlotte, but our marriage—it *is* a kind of marriage—is one of like minds, of time. Our guilt and forgiveness is not peripheral or muted or secret. Charlotte and I have an understanding, and we live in it without borders.

But, I saw his dilemma, and sympathized. I know what a sad thing it is to feel you have betrayed someone dear. That another's disappointment originates with your mistakes. That who you really are is, perhaps, after all, not good enough.

Sitting with Earl in the tiny smoking lounge, a monologue of insight and advice was forming in my mind. I wanted to say, you know, all you need is a little faith, Earl. Mildred will have it in her to forgive you. She will feel hint, she'll be angry, I wanted to explain, but it's something you'll have to go through together. She'll need all that much more reassurance, it will be difficult for her to trust. An idea about what the marriage was, or was supposed to be...it has been challenged now, and changed.

But, what do I know about marriage? I just leaned a bit closer to him, and we looked in each other's eyes. "Maybe she'll forgive you."

"But, if my wife finds out about this...." Earl stammered quickly, locking his fingers together tight, licking his lips.

Again, I am a witness. I saw the pain of his predicament— it was really not at all about fidelity, or even about the feelings or future of Mildred and Earl. This big, gentle man was caught in a moment, frozen by a choice he had made and by a great, powerful fear he had not known before. I was embarrassed and tense, and thought about what Charlotte always says: People tell such awful stories.

"If my wife finds out," he said, slow and soft, dejected, but with chilling certainty, "I just know that nothing will ever be the same."

Fourteen

Yesterday, when I put my key in the latch I thought: What if the impossible has happened? I'll step in and the house will be empty; there will be a note from Charlotte saying she has moved away. Goodbye, I am all over my troubles now and have gone on a cruise...or fallen in love or got a job or decided to live in the city with Annie. What if Charlotte has disappeared? But, Charlotte was home, seated at that worn and unsteady dining table, working a crossword puzzle. Her smile was brilliant as she rushed to hug me.

Today, I guess I am feeling that familiar, hardly serious fury toward Charlotte. The kitchen sink is filled with all the cups and saucers and spoons. But, it's more than that. It's the radio or television always on, sometimes both of them, and her scraps of paper, her drawings, books just skimmed through and left open on every table and chair. So often, she'll say: "I really have to straighten this place up," but her version of straightening is to push things from one surface to another, into a corner, off to the side; and then she just turns out all the lights.

But it's even more than that. It's her arrogant, insistent serenity; she seems to live without needs.

I have been feeling so much healthier, stronger, and I phoned Dr Decker for the results of my latest blood tests: they indicate the immediate danger has passed. Dr Decker told me the current belief about AIDS is that it may become, for more people, a chronic illness, a manageable condition, like diabetes. He was trying to be reassuring; in fact, he sounded optimistic. But, for me it was only a voice on a phone saying, it looks like maybe you won't die for a while yet. A daily reprieve.

I find myself longing for a trip into the city—for a ride on the train, to the library, to the cafe, even to see Jesse—but I'm not recuperated enough to engage in my old, normal life.

This morning I began work on my manuscript, trying to decipher

Mr Cole's huge, slanting scrawl. Charlotte was busy on the floor a few feet from my desk, with three or four books open before her. Now she is convinced that she has psychic powers and is studying witchcraft, voodoo, clairvoyance and other things paranormal. This special sense of hers, she says, explains her abhorrence of the outside world. She actually can see the inevitable doom as a black and grey vapor hanging above all the ignorant people's heads, or something along those lines.

The phone rang, and I welcomed the interruption. Before I answered, I was aware that Charlotte abruptly stopped fiddling with her scissors and photographs; she was watching me.

"Yes?" I said. "Oh, yes. Mr Cole's secretary. Ms Wharton, right?"

Charlotte breathed a soft sigh.

Vera had been crying obviously, for she sniffled after every couple of words. Otherwise, she was utterly professional and blunt. She told me she regretted having to intrude, she knew I had been sick recently. "That's really all right, I'm feeling fairly well," I said, and was about to tell her that my prognosis, at least for the short term, was promising. But, Vera went on: XXX Press, Inc. would not be able after all to publish my novel, but it had nothing to do with the quality of the work itself, in fact Mr Cole had been most enthusiastic about it. XXX Press, Inc. unfortunately and suddenly had had to file for bankruptcy. Its funds were no longer available. Mr Cole had asked Vera to inform me of this development and offer his sincere apologies, his best hopes for finding another publisher, and to say that if he can be of any help in the future I should not hesitate to call.

I was silenced, shocked as much by the formality of her words and tone as by what she had to say. And then I heard her blow her nose with a mighty honk and she departed from this heaviness, was almost whining: "It's just so awful that small publishing companies, the ones who take risks, experiment, explore, we go out of business left and right, while the big guys with their silly sex dramas and thrillers and horror books...." she trailed off. Then, almost hostile: "God knows if Kafka would ever even see print in these times." Vera composed herself. "Mr Cole and, I might add, myself as well, are very sorry to disappoint you."

"I appreciate your calling me, Vera."

"Quite all right."

We hung up.

Charlotte, of course, had sensed some trouble at the first ring of the phone, and was almost gleeful to find her premonition confirmed. "I *knew* it was bad news. Something about the book."

For my part, I was not surprised at this development, and for several pretentious moments keenly felt a broad resentment toward the powers of ignorance and conservatism, on behalf of both Kafka and myself. Charlotte wondered what kind of job Vera Wharton would be able to find now.

Charlotte is doing what she can. My first night home she called out: "Supper's on," and it was a plate of grey-brown, lumpy gravy over rice and a bowl of watermelon sections.

Later, she came to my room—she has not stepped a foot in my room for years—with a book of stories to read aloud. Charlotte's voice is hoarse, but lively; her pauses and breaths, her pace is so familiar and dear to me, like a favorite nursery rhyme.

" 'During the whole of a dull, dark, and soundless day in the autumn of the year, when the clouds hung oppressively low in the heavens, I had been passing alone, on horseback, through a singularly dreary tract of country; and at length found myself, as the shades of the evening drew on, within view of the melancholy House of Usher.' "

The room was dim: just one lamp by her chair and her lighted cigarette which bounced each time she turned a page. It was a sweet night; I passed into a dreamless sleep.

A few days later I was well enough to sit in the kitchen. It is finally spring. Islands of melting snow and ice dot the yard. I was grateful to be home.

We each had a section of the newspaper, and I read from the *Dear Margie* column: "Dear Margie. I have been married twenty-nine years and recently had a very brief affair. I have ended it, but this woman is threatening to expose me. I adore my wife. I am terrified she will be so hurt and angry that she will leave me. What should I do? Signed, Desperate."

Charlotte took a gulp of coffee. She is bored with tea these days. "How ridiculous. It's the trap of marriage, it's a built-in trap." She sounded angry. "Because we don't...oh, what am I trying to say?" she asked me.

119

I was not eager to pursue this conversation, or to listen to Charlotte's relentless moralizing. "Here's one of your serial killers, Charlotte. Should I cut out the article?"

But she went on: "Marriage is this very sinister myth that no one can live up to, so they rely on the promise, the promise. And it is never fulfilled unless you lie to each other."

I held my robe tighter at my neck. I was so impatient for one of my walks, again to be on a road I know.

"All I know—" she paused, twisted a bit of her hair with a finger, and was suddenly gentler. "You can't deceive someone about who you really are. You must not let anything take the place of love. You must tell the truth. That's love."

Because Charlotte is Charlotte, because she is a delicate, fragile creature, I forget sometimes how strong is her foundation: it's granite, centuries-old, cunning. Because I feel sadly put-upon by a helpless, untidy Charlotte, I often forget and am shocked breathless when I see her wisdom. I really envy and really resent that Charlotte does not seem to care; so, in the moments when it is clear that Charlotte does care, and with such depth and sorrow, it is like I've fallen joyously, brilliantly in love. And I'm never sure what Charlotte means—her language is like scraps of paper with words tossed in the air, and when they float to the ground and have formed phrases, there is her truth—but, I know within it all, she is saying she loves me.

Charlotte plucked a grapefruit section between her finger and thumb and popped it into her mouth. We were quiet, then. Charlotte became suddenly interested in the gossip column and I watched her follow the lines with her finger.

"Charlotte? What would be your advice to Desperate?"

"Well, of course he must tell his wife. Just say he is sorry, or whatever, that he didn't mean to hurt her, or whatever. It isn't important, is it? But, he must tell the truth. He must tell the truth because...well, because it's the truth." She gave a short, quick, firm nod and grabbed another page of the paper. It was the obituary listings, and Charlotte remarked on the passing of a well-known and eccentric older woman poet named Glass. I looked over Charlotte's shoulder. The item did not say how Ms Glass had died.

"Suicide, I bet," said Charlotte. "Things probably just got too much for her." In this instance, Charlotte may be right.

▼

There was something strikingly different about Aunt Kaye when she was here this morning to drop off Charlotte's bank statement. It was that her lips were not so pursed, her shoulders not so tense. Charlotte noticed it, too, immediately.

"So," said Aunt Kaye when we were all at the kitchen table. "Charlotte, what about this burial plot business?" The arrangements for Charlotte's death have long concerned Aunt Kaye, she routinely brings the subject up; but, even with this, today her heart did not seem in it, she was not quite her usual macabre self.

"Aunt Kaye?" Charlotte lowered her head, smiled, peered at her aunt. "Is there something on your mind?"

Aunt Kaye laughed, short and loud. It was utterly shocking to hear her laugh. "What? On my mind?"

"Oh," Charlotte said, gathering the tea things together, "I'm mistaken then. I just thought—"

"Well." Aunt Kaye looked at me, then at the edge of the table. When she grinned and bit her lip, Charlotte and I exchanged a glance which meant we had to know whatever this news was. "Well," said Aunt Kaye, "I really don't want the word to get around, *obviously, for obvious* reasons. But—" she straightened her head and looked directly at Charlotte—"I'm pregnant, dear," and she gave a little jump.

Charlotte nearly fell into her chair. I lit a cigarette.

The story is simply that Aunt Kaye has wanted to be pregnant, desired the experience, wished to raise a child and, furthermore, believes she'll be an extraordinarily competent and loving mother. So, she arranged it. As to the father: "A very sweet person I've known many years. We'll get married, of course." But, he seems not to be of primary importance.

As she was leaving, she hugged Charlotte, she even hugged me. She told me she was so glad to hear things weren't too serious and that I was feeling better. She almost left that giant pocketbook of hers behind, and then laughed heartily at her absent-mindedness, and Charlotte and I

121

were both just stunned and delighted by this new development.

"You never know about people, do you?" she said. "You never know what goes on in people's minds, do you?"

I must have watched Charlotte, silently, for quite a while, for the morning sun passed through our kitchen, across her deep black hair and thin, blushed cheeks. She was looking out the window. Is it possible that her interest was piqued by Aunt Kaye's bold move, that Charlotte herself is ever tantalized with the idea of motherhood? I suppose not. Holding life, bearing it, nurturing and raising it—these must be as frightening to Charlotte as anything else.

When I was a little boy, it seemed a tiny, tender world, and my cares were the buttons on my shirt, the names of my toy animals, the simple schedule of meals and naps. School loomed ahead, a menace; I was afraid, but I knew I would have Charlotte.

I remember a lot of whispering. Our mothers together on the sofa, very serious. Or Mother and Dad with the door closed after supper, and she would emerge to tell me to take a bath, and then he would come later and say it was time for bed.

One New Year's night Charlotte and I were sitting on the window-seat in my father's study. We were in our pyjamas, but Charlotte wore her play nurse's cap as well. "You just keep watching," Charlotte told me, "and you'll see everything change when the new year comes. Everything just shifts, moves, a little bit."

Where was my father? Was he angry about something? Sometimes he did get angry about things. And Mother was in the front room, alone, on a pillow before the fire.

"It's coming soon, keep watching," ordered Charlotte. She was so bossy, then.

I called to my mother: "Is it really coming soon? Is it really almost time?" Just her back, her head lowered, she was leaning on one arm, her legs were tucked under her. I rose and walked toward her. I went to her side. She would not look at me, she would not lift her head.

"Why are you crying? What's the matter?"

She was painted with the soft orange light of the fire, but she did not look pretty. She looked worn, sad. She touched my hair. "Nothing, nothing. It's only that it's New Years."

I went slowly across our old light green carpet, dragging the feet of my pyjamas, back to the perch with Charlotte.

"She's crying, Charlotte. Do you know why she's crying?" Charlotte kept her face pressed to the window. Her breath fogged the pane and she quickly wiped it clear. "She's crying because being a grownup woman is the hardest, saddest thing you can be."

▼

Last night, late, I was sleeping soundly, and heard my name called. I stumbled over a pile of magazines on my way to Charlotte's room, and as I reached her door, she was calling my name again. Those bad dreams of hers, I thought....

I pushed open the door and she was sitting in bed, fully awake, grinning, blinking. The room was lit by candles. Her ancient record player was at the end of her bed, and the needle was skipping.

Between all her toes and all her fingers were wads of cotton. Bottles of nail polish and remover were on her night stand. Her nails were ruby red—but not only her nails; crimson blotches and drips and smears were on her arms, her hands, her knees. She looked like she'd been attacked by a pack of hungry little mice.

"Oh, God, were you sleeping?" she asked.

Because I was breathing hard, my robe was open, my hair was mussed, and I was leaning into that room poised for rescue, cued for a crisis.

She said: "Oh, I'm sorry. It's just...I can't get up. I had this idea to paint my nails. And then the record started to skip." She was holding back until I laughed first. "See, I didn't realise you were sleeping. I guess I lost track of how late it was. So I called out." The rhythmical thumping of the dusty needle in the grooves filled a long silence.

"I'm so sorry," she said. "Really, I am, I'm sorry."

I was pouting, cranky. I answered sarcastically: "Yes, well, I forgive you." I moved towards the record player, intending to slap its arm and send it scratching across the record.

"It's Ethel Merman," Charlotte said.

And then we did laugh, both of us, and I put the needle on the record and we sang along—Charlotte louder, with more delight and abandon, more certain of the lyrics; I, self-consciously but singing, singing nonetheless.

In olden days, a glimpse of stocking
Was looked on as something shocking
Now heaven knows
Anything goes
Good authors, too, who once knew better words
Now only use four-letter words
When writing prose
Anything goes
The world has gone mad today
And good's bad today
And black's white today
And day's night today
And most guys today
That women prize today
Are just silly gigolos
So though I'm not a great romancer
I know that you're bound to answer
When I propose
Anything goes

▼

Today, a perfect walk, like some gorgeous dream. Each shadow I saw or shiver I felt was mnemonic, like a chord of music can be, or a fragrance. Our town washed through me, cleaned me out.

Mrs Turner was in front of the post office holding the hand of her sickly little girl, Rose, whose bonnet crookedly framed her pinched face. Peg Pelliteer—can her hair be a shade lighter?—was talking about the meanest man she'd ever seen. "Now this man was cold sober. He happened to work right over here at Peerless Manufacturing. And he had this sweetie-pie little daughter named Mandy or something who had braids. Anyway, I saw this fella pull this little Mandy up by the neck and rattle her like she was a toy doll. Her face went purple. Choked her almost to death. Then he just tossed her down like nothing. And this Mandy or whatever was writhing around and beet-faced and screaming—well, no wonder! Now, that is the *meanest* man I *ever* saw in my *whole* life."

By this time, Rose was crying and Mrs Turner's face had gone ash-colored. I walked by. I had no business at the post office today.

Mrs Coffee was in her usual jam with the Cadillac. I stood far back from the curb and smoked half a cigarette, waiting until she'd done her maneuvering.

I passed the factory just as its noon whistle blew and the women pushed through the side door to feel some sun and complain and laugh. And my God, after all this time and the seasons, that assemblage of grotesque gloppy garbage still sits, untouched, circled by huge flies and now crowned by a rusty scrap of metal. The man with the coffee cart rolls right past it, whistling.

When I reached Hornstein's store I tapped on the window.

"Yes?" Mr Hornstein peered through the screen. "Oh, yes. Hello, hello. You're home, you're up and around. Good, good, good. All better, are you?"

"Yes. I seem to be all right for now."

"That's good. You'll come in for a glass of juice maybe? David's gone out, he said he felt like having a swim." I followed Mr Hornstein inside the damp, cluttered store. "I said, 'David, you think it's summer already?' I said, 'You'll freeze to death.' But...so he goes anyhow."

Mr Hornstein poured me apple juice in a paper cup, and I leaned against the counter. We had little to say to each other really, but there was no awkwardness or tension in the moments we stood there.

"So, what is happening with this book?" he asked. I love that Mr Hornstein looks directly at me, seems so serious and interested.

"Well, it looks like it won't be published very soon, I'm sorry to say. The company went out of business."

"Isn't that terrible? Oh, people care all about these crazy television actresses and the big sports players—but what happens to a writer? So, listen. It's a good book, it's going to get printed. This, I'm positive of."

I shrugged, smiled. I thanked Mr Hornstein for the juice. I told him I was eager to get on with my walk around town, it had been so long. He patted me on the shoulder. It was a genuine touch; the slender fingers were old, steadfast, truthful ones.

125

Pain disassembles us; but we are put back together finally, I think, and healed by our suffering.

Isn't that why there is such glory in war, and people see hope and beauty in sickness? Or am I being suckered in by cliche sentimentalism?

I walked up the hill, just to the edge of the woods, where I could look over the town. I saw the roof of our house, the flagpole, the tower of the fire station; under the fading sun it seemed colored by light from one of those old lanterns. A spectacular view, a perfect spot. I must tell Charlotte about that view.

I stood on a bed of frozen, purple and brown leaves. The river was still. Tall, slim yellow weeds bent gracefully over the bank. A rowboat, its paint cracked and worn, was overturned and rested against the unsteady, grey wooden wharf.

Because what really keeps me with Charlotte—attached to her—is her knowledge, within her ineffable and deep sorrow, that even now, life is so precious.

I spotted something white. I stepped forward to see. It was not a bird, it was not a bit of newspaper blown across the river's surface.

There... some thing white...and a splash. A naked man in the water.

As he lifted up for a breath and shook wet, blue-black hair away from his eyes, strong shoulders and a back appeared, and then were gone within a spray of foam, and under the muddy green the body glided soundlessly.

I kept watch. For a second or two, I would lose sight of the figure altogether, and then hear the water, see the movement I knelt, so as not to be seen myself. I pressed my fingers to my lips.

The man floated on his back for a moment, then rolled, pushed himself through a wave of twigs and leaves, towards the wharf.

▼

He holds the edge of the dock and swings his legs up. He stands facing the bank. He stretches his arms over his head, locking fingers, and is meticulous and graceful with his motion, expanding the chest, straining his ribs and thighs, rolling his head in a circle each way. He seems to be trying to break free of his body; of all the tension in its joints, grief in its muscles, disappointment and desire stuck in the veins, the awesome taboos lodged in all the cells.

From so far above, I can see clearly this bare, white, perfect form. I take a breath—deeper, cleaner than my usual breaths. And it is like I *am* a child again—not merely bullied or caressed by memory, not making up a story, to run and tell Charlotte.

I *am* a child again.

My huge eyes stay fixed and loyal and hopeful.

Now I am not tormented by someone else's scars from years ago, or concessions or apologies or betrayal or dread. Now I am forgiven and free. Here, now, before the blessed conjurer disappears again, I am able to witness the finest aspects of this most mysterious and wondrous magic trick; and for a charmed second, know I will see the solution.

The Library of Homosexual Congress, an imprint of Rebel Satori Press, preserves and promotes classic and provocative works of gay literature and nonfiction, with focuses on the AIDS crisis, the nascent gay rights movement as well as irreverent works of sexual culture and groundbreaking titles that deserve renewed attention.

Curated by Tom Cardamone and Sven Davisson